Jake

Cowboy Rendezvous, Volume 2

Lori Wilde

Published by Lori Wilde, 2022.

Table of Contents

Chapter One

Jake Strickland pushed the heavy, black-framed glasses up on his nose, and peered through the nonprescription lenses at the PowerPoint presentation projected on the wall of the main tiki hut.

The infuriating glasses kept sliding down, and it was all he could do to keep himself from yanking them off and flinging them across the room.

Playing the undercover role of orchid-loving geek was harder than it looked, especially when he was a dyed-in-the-wool cowboy and longed for his Stetson, Wranglers and cowboy boots.

"You know what they say about the amore orchid?" Bunk Jones, the seventy-ish guy sitting next to him, asked in a low voice.

Bunk was dressed much like Jake. The older man wore a Hawaiian-print shirt, khaki cargo pants, pocket protector filled with colored pens and hiking boots.

The old feller had yapped at him on the long bus ride in from the San Jose airport and apparently Bunk had decided they were gonna be bosom buddies.

Jake had done his best to shake the guy, but it was a small group of intellectuals, and there weren't too many places to hide in the Costa Rican compound.

Jake didn't ask for him to elaborate, but Bunk told him anyway. "Legend has it that the amore orchid emits such potent pheromones that whenever you smell it, you have an irresistible urge to make love."

"What?" Jake jerked his head around and stared at Bunk.

"Yep, it's true."

"So, this orchid is like what? Floral Viagra?"

Bunk shrugged and grinned slyly. "I dunno, I'm just sayin'..."

"Is that why you're here?"

Jake didn't want to think about Bunk on the prowl for a girlfriend, but he supposed old dudes needed love, too. Hey, Jake himself didn't have a romantic partner. He'd been going through a dry spell of late, and this nerdy getup, and unkempt hair, wasn't helping matters.

"Is that so wrong?" Bunk smirked.

"Far be it from me to judge." Jake raised his palms. "We've all got our reasons to be on this trip."

Some nobler than others.

"What can I say? I like studious, scientific women, and they gravitate toward these kind of things." Bunk waved a hand.

Was Bunk using the orchid-hunting group as a dating service? Novel idea. He might be onto something. Jake scanned the scant pickings and shrugged. To each his own.

"What about that one over there?" Bunk used his chin to point at a woman in her mid-twenties sitting on a stool at the front of the building beside the podium. "She looks interesting."

The young woman was dressed in a style that Jake would only describe as *mitts-off-the-merchandise buster.*

She had on baggy black jeans, a gray T-shirt with *Columbia* printed across the front, and a pair of hiking boots. Her hair was jet-black and fell to her shoulders, Cleopatra-style. She wore skinny, red-framed rectangular glasses and no jewelry. Her skin was notebook-paper pale. A sheen of pink lip gloss rode her lips, and her mascara was the same color as her hair. Her eyes, from what he could see of them behind those glasses, were dark navy blue.

Weirdly, his pulse skittered, but why? She was not his type.

"She's too young for you," he said.

"Not for me. I got my eyes on Lucinda." Bunk nodded at a silver-haired woman in the first row. "I meant for you."

"Nah."

"Why not? You in a relationship?"

"No way. I'm footloose and fancy-free and intend on staying that way."

"Ahh."

"Ahh what?"

Bunk smiled. "You're one of *those*."

It seemed like an indictment, and this from a coot old enough to be Jake's grandfather if he had one.

"I'm one of what?" Jake asked.

"The love 'em and leave 'em kind."

Jake was about to argue, but then he shut his mouth. He didn't intentionally set out to love 'em and leave 'em, but whenever a woman started talking about taking their relationship to the next level—i.e., commitment—Jake's feet got twitchy.

"You're right," Bunk said. "She is too much woman for you."

"Who? Emo girl?"

"Emo?" Bunk looked confused.

"Never mind. What makes you think she's too much woman for me?"

"Woman like that..." Bunk bobbed his head as if he knew everything. "She needs a man who'll stick around and find out exactly what's going on in that brain of hers. She's sharp as a tack. You can see that right off the bat."

Bunk had a point. Jake stared at emo girl.

At that moment, she raised her head.

Their gazes met, and for one second, he could have sworn he saw surprise in her eyes, as if she knew him, but in an instant, the look was gone, and she glared like he was getting on her last nerve.

Jake was the first one to break eye contact. Not his usual MO.

"Yep." Bunk cackled. "She's too much woman for the likes of Mr. Love 'Em and Leave 'Em."

"Stop calling me that."

"Hey, if the shoe fits..." Bunk lifted his shoulders. "Me, I'm going to talk to Lucinda."

And then the old man was gone, ambling down the grass aisle to the front row. Bunk leaned in to say something to Lucinda, who smiled up at him and scooted over so he could take the seat next to her.

Jake had to give the old dude props for his fast moves.

Just then, a man stalked through the back door of the tiki hut and up to the podium. He looked efficient and professorial.

"Hello, I'm Dr. Hampton, head of the Botany department at Columbia University." He put a hand toward emo girl. "And this is my number one research assistant, Madison Garrett. She's doing her doctoral dissertation on the amore orchid."

Madison raised a hand, and she smiled at the group, but when her eyes met his again, the welcoming smile disappeared.

What? She didn't like him? Huh. That was unusual. Women almost always liked him. At least until they figured out that he wasn't in it for the long haul.

Professor Hampton went into detail about the research project he and his team were engaged in. They wanted to find the amore orchid—which was assumed to exist only in Costa Rica—and get it listed on the endangered species list.

If the group found out that Jake was working for an orchid collector in Taiwan, his goose would be cooked, and he'd end up on the wrong side of a botanical mob.

Clearly, these people took their orchids seriously. He didn't get what the big deal was. It was just a flower. Jake had no real vested interest in the orchid itself. All he cared about saving Deke's ranch.

Two weeks ago, Tao Liu had approached Jake at the Lazy Daze Dude Ranch where he trained cutting horses and told him about Professor Hampton's Costa Rican expedition. Lui had often sent Jake around the world to evaluate, buy, and train cutting horses for him. And he'd sent Jake to Costa Rica two other times on his quest for the best of the best.

But this was the first time Liu had asked him to do something non-horse related.

Initially, Jake had said no to orchid smuggling. He knew the billionaire businessman had his fingers in all kinds of pies—some legit, some not so much—and he hadn't wanted to get involved in anything shady, or crossways with the law, but a large chunk of his income came from Liu, and he'd had to walk a tight line.

And then Liu made an offer Jake couldn't refuse.

Go get the amore orchid or Liu was calling in the note on the Lazy Daze, which would not only leave Jake unemployed, but worse, it would rob his surrogate father, Deke Kahill, of his livelihood and the dude ranch that had been in Deke's family for four generations. The ranch meant everything to Deke, and to Jake himself. He'd grown up there.

When Jake was a twelve-year-old runaway, Deke had taken him off the streets and given him a home at the Lazy Daze. He'd cut his teeth on horses. Deke had given Jake both a home and a profession.

He couldn't allow Liu to hang Deke out to dry. The rancher was family. It was time for Jake to give back to the only person who'd ever really believed in him.

Forced into a corner, Jake had agreed to Liu's proposition with a great deal of reservation. If he succeeded, Liu would forgive Deke's debt and the Lazy Daze would be safe from liquidation. If he failed...

Well, Liu had left those consequences dangling, leaving Jake to assume Liu would foreclose on the ranch if Jake couldn't produce the amore orchid.

He had one option.

Succeed.

And he wasn't about to let anything get in his way. If that meant cozying up with Miss Madison Garrett, so be it. He had to get his hands on that orchid, come hell or high water.

The idea of befriending Madison wasn't repulsive. Beneath the nerdy glasses and frumpy clothes, she was kind of hot. Full mouth. Long dark lashes. Straight white teeth. Intense dark blue eyes.

"The amore orchid is very rare, and there are collectors who will stop at nothing to have one, and that includes hiring soldiers of fortune to beat us to the punch."

Bunk raised a hand. "To what end?"

"To steal them," Professor Hampton said.

"Why?" Lucinda asked.

"Money," Professor Hampton said. "The amore orchid is priceless."

Jake forced himself not to slink down in his seat. No one knew why he was here, and he didn't want to give anyone a reason to ask him hard questions.

THE LECTURE ENDED, and the group immediately gravitated to the wine and cheese buffet set up on one side of the hut.

Madison stood awkwardly in the corner, making her obligatory appearance and waiting for the chance to escape to the quiet of her hut.

She hated these glad-handing meet-and-greets. Luckily, most of the volunteers were over fifty. She often felt more comfortable in the company of senior citizens.

Although...

There was one guy near her own age. He wore rectangular-framed glasses that were almost identical to the ones she had on, except where hers were red, his were black. His hair was shaggy, unkempt, and a pocket protector filled with pens peeked from his shirt pocket.

Nothing suspicious about any of that. Almost every male in the place—including her professor—looked similarly.

No, what stuck out about this guy was the way he carried himself. Not slump-shouldered and shy like many introverts she knew, but with razor-straight shoulders, almost military in stance. He also possessed a sly grin and a way of moving that shouted, *I'm the cock of the walk.*

This guy was more than he appeared. Was he playing at being a nerdy geek? But why? Hmm. Red flag?

Orchid thief.

The thought sent goosebumps over her arm. But what orchid thief would be so bold as to infiltrate their group?

Blowing out her breath, Madison put a smile on her face and strolled over. Should she treat him like the introvert he seemed to be or just shoot for the ego he couldn't quite cover up? In the end, her own timidity won out.

"Hi," she said.

A slow, easy grin started at one side of his mouth and slipped to the other, and his eyes held onto hers like sticky glue.

Oh, yeah, there was something off about this guy.

But then he quickly dropped his gaze, ducked his head, toed the ground, and mumbled, "Hello."

"I'm Madison," she said and thrust out her hand.

"Um...so I heard..." He averted his gaze but reached for her hand.

The second their palms touched, a shot of pure sexual awareness spread down his arms and traveled up hers.

The sensation was electric. She'd felt nothing like it before.

His eyes widened, and he looked as thrown as she felt. Quickly, they both dropped their hands. He stuck his in the pockets of his cargo shorts. She clasp hers behind her back.

They stood there, focusing on everything but each other. Finally, Madison hooked one arm around the other. "What's your name?"

"Jake. Jake Strickland." He pushed his glasses up.

This time she noticed his work-roughened hands. From gardening? Peering into his eyes, she felt a strange ping in the pit of her stomach.

He smiled.

She couldn't help smiling back.

This wasn't normal for her. She wasn't spontaneous woman. Much less someone who would fall into lust easily, but she couldn't stop her gaze from tracking over his muscular shoulders—so non-geekish—to his broad chest, lean waist, narrow hips and...

She jerked her gaze away. *For heaven's sake, Madison, don't stare at the man's crotch.* "Well, Jake Strickland, it's nice to meet you."

"Nice to meet you as well, Maddie Garrett."

"It's not Maddie. It's Madison. No one calls me Maddie."

"Why not?"

"I don't like it."

"Why not?"

"What are you? Three years old?"

"Just curious about you."

"No," she said. "We're not here for that."

He chuckled.

Taken aback, Maddie gave him a look. "What's so funny?"

"Your intensity."

"That's funny?"

"Not funny, no," he said, backpedaling. "I just find your passion charming."

"Are you flirting with me?" Madison's belly churned. She couldn't decide whether to be attracted to him or suspicious.

"Would it irritate you if I said yes?"

"Yes."

"Okay then, I'm not flirting with you." He winked.

She frowned. "Are you fully prepared for tomorrow? Do you honestly understand what you've gotten yourself into?"

"Yep."

"Packed?"

"Yep."

"Got bug spray?"

"Yep."

"Flashlight? Sunscreen?"

"Yep. Yep."

"First aid kit? Utility knife? Rain poncho?"

"Yep, yep, yep."

"Can you say anything besides 'yep'?"

"Yep." He was teasing her, and she couldn't decide if she liked it or not.

"We leave at dawn." She didn't know why she was hanging around this guy, baiting him. She had a mountain of work that needed her attention.

"I'll be ready."

"The hike is arduous."

"Duly noted."

"Please double check your supplies, Mr. Yeppers," she said, softening. "It can get pretty hairy out there."

"I've been in a few jungles." He lowered his eyelashes and widened his grin. "I know what I'm getting into."

"Do you?"

"I'm a guy who thrives on challenges."

Now *that* sounded one hundred percent cocky. Not at all like something an anxious nerd would say.

Red flag number two.

She narrowed her eyes and was about to interrogate him about his jungle experience, orchid thieves were a legitimate concern, but he preempted her.

"See you in the morning, *Maddie.*" He turned and walked away, leaving Madison more irritated, confused, and attracted to him than ever.

Chapter Two

J ake ducked around the corner of the hut and let out a long-held breath.

He had to be careful with Madison Garrett. She was as sharp as a shark's tooth and playing at being a nerd didn't come easily to him.

By nature, he was a self-confident guy who normally took the lead with a woman when he was interested.

It had required every bit of willpower he possessed to pretend to be shy and retiring. Jake didn't think he'd been all that successful at convincing her. Especially there at the end, when she'd been shooting him eye-daggers.

Bunk was right about one thing. Pulling the wool over Madison's eyes wouldn't be a piece of cake.

Jake paced outside the main tiki hut, planning for the trek ahead of them. If they did find the orchid, how could he steal it without being caught?

Everyone else was still lingering over drinks, nibbles, and conversations about rare orchids. The encampment was surrounded by mountainous jungle terrain. Madison was right. An orchid hunt was not for the faint of heart.

He should head to his tent to started packing and get some sleep, but he was edgy and restless. Something didn't sit right with Jake, and he couldn't quite put his finger on what it was.

Just then, Professor Hampton and Madison emerged from the back flap of the tent. They stood some distance from Jake, and he couldn't hear what they were saying. But in the glow from the flickering tiki torches, he could see the strain on Madison's face. It seemed she and her mentor were arguing.

Hmm, what was this?

Keeping to the shadows, Jake crept closer.

"Based on my calculations," Madison said, "you're off the mark, Professor."

"No, you're wrong." Dr. Hampton shook his head vigorously.

Madison spouted intricate scientific mumbo jumbo about pH balance and soil conditions, optimum temperature range, and daylight hours. Intrigued, Jake edged ever nearer.

"Listen to me. The amore orchid is most likely growing on the northern slopes above the San Pablo waterfall," she said.

"Your calculations are inexact since every species of orchid has its own specific conditions for optimal germination. Plus, native folklore has the amore orchid growing far south of the San Pablo waterfall," Professor Hampton argued.

Apparently, there was some tension between the teacher and his student. Jake rubbed his chin pensively.

Madison sank her hands on her hips. "You said you would give my input serious consideration."

"I did, and I've decided you're wrong."

Anger crept into her voice. "I don't understand how you can dismiss my work so cavalierly. I have spent three years of my life on this research and—"

"We don't have the time or manpower to go gallivanting off on your wild-goose chase, Madison. Our resources are limited."

"Wait just a minute." She glowered, and her voice turned suspicious. "Is this about last summer?"

"Of course not." Dr. Hampton sounded indignant.

"It is! You're mad because I broke things off with you, and now you're punishing me for it."

"Don't be ridiculous." Dr. Hampton snorted.

"You said we were both adults, and that you could still work with me without letting your feelings get in the way. I took you at your word."

"Our little fling meant nothing to me," Dr. Hampton said. "Get over yourself."

Ouch.

So, Hampton and his research assistant had hooked up last summer, and now this horse's ass was taking it out on her when things went south. Jake felt a twinge of sympathy for the woman.

In the light from the full moon, Madison looked mad enough to rip open a coconut with her bare hands.

Man, she was fierce. Jake felt a pleasant stirring inside him. A sizzle that started in his stomach and spread downward.

"If you take your group south, you won't find a damn thing," she said. "I can guarantee you that."

"What do you mean, *your* group?" Dr. Hampton scowled. "It's *our* group."

"Not anymore, it's not. I've spent my entire adult life looking for the amore orchid, and I will not be disappointed again. Not when I'm so close. I'm going north to San Pablo. You're free to follow me if you want; otherwise, I'll see you back here in a week."

With that parting shot, Madison turned on her heels, ducked her head, and started stalking toward Jake so quickly that he didn't have time to get out of her way.

She ran smack-dab into his chest.

The collision forced all the air from Jake's lungs. "*Oof.*"

She'd bowled him over. Literally.

He was lying on the ground, and she was on top of him, straddling his torso. He blinked up at her. She stared down at him.

He saw in her eyes the same baffled attraction that he felt.

Madison uttered an unladylike curse word and sprang to her feet. "What were you doing prowling around in the dark, Strickland?"

"I wasn't prowling." He lied flat out and levered himself to his feet. He splayed a palm on his stomach. Was it pitching because of their impact or because of the full-body contact with Madison?

Maybe a little of both.

They stood glaring at each other, neither one of them moving.

"Madison!" Professor Hampton's voice was sharp in the darkness. "Get back over here. We have to discuss the logistics of separate expeditions."

"You're being summoned," Jake said.

She swallowed but didn't look away. Her gaze drilled into his. "Coming, Dr. Hampton."

Rattled by the chemistry surging between them, Jake shifted his weight. "You gotta come, I gotta go."

"Huh?"

He heard how that sounded, winced, tried to backtrack. "You gotta go, I've gotta come." Hell, he'd just made things worse. "I mean—"

"Get to your tent." Madison pointed toward the volunteers' accommodations.

Bossy. He kind of liked that.

"I want to come with you," he said, meaning he wanted to be part of her expedition, but under the circumstances, it had a completely different meaning.

She gave him a go-straight-to-hell expression.

"What I meant to say—"

"I know what you meant to say."

"So, can I? Come?"

"Stop using that word."

"Which word?" He couldn't resist teasing her.

"You know which word."

"Come?"

"Stop saying it."

He pantomimed zipping his lip, but he was laughing too hard to carry it off.

"Madison?" Dr. Hampton called again.

She cast an assessing glance over Jake. "Be packed and ready to go. I'll meet you in the cantina hut at six a.m. If you're not there, I'm leaving without you."

Then she spun on her heels and stalked away in the darkness. That's when he knew for sure she liked him, too.

WHY HAD SHE AGREED to take that weirdo Jake Strickland into the jungle with her?

Madison stared at herself in the small camp mirror as she brushed her teeth and got ready for bed. Especially after she'd caught him eavesdropping on the fight she'd had with Hampton.

Red flag number three.

But even though she was sure her calculations on where to find the orchid were correct, the idea of venturing into the ruggedly tropical terrain on her own scared the pants off her. She was a scholar, not an adventurer.

There might be something off about Strickland, but he looked to be as adventuresome as they came and in excellent physical condition to boot.

Unfortunately, she felt a bizarre attraction toward him.

Okay, maybe the attraction wasn't so inexplicable. He had a miles of muscles, all firm and honed. A strong jaw just begging to be stroked. Eyes the color of charcoal. A roguish broken nose that added to, rather than detracted from, his sex appeal. And besides all that, he smelled good too.

Thank heavens she'd made a "summer-of-no-sex-bet" with her three best friends, Bianca, Izzy and Emma. They'd all had miserable flings the previous summer and declared this one sex-free and put money down to prove they were serious.

Not only did Madison need the money from the bet to finish her research, but wager should quell her interest in Jake Strickland. She couldn't afford the distraction of a man like him.

Because Strickland was surely that with his lanky, rock hard body and cowboy drawl.

So why are you talking him with you?

Good question. Maybe she wouldn't. Maybe he wouldn't even show up in time.

Madison crawled into her sleeping bag, wearing the silky lingerie designed by Tomaz Santos. She'd brought the sexy garment as a reminder to stay celebrate and also to do market research for her friend, Bianca, who was working on an ad campaign for the lingerie.

She tried not to notice how the underwear caressed her skin. It was so silky and luxurious. Not something she was accustomed to wearing. Madison also tried her best not to think about Jake and his roughened hands slipping beneath the waistband of the panties...

Stop it!

Right. Head in the game. She was in the middle of a turf war with her professor. If she was going to fret about something, that's what she should fret about.

She'd known the fling she and Hampton had last summer had been a big mistake. They'd been in Belize, hunting down a lead on an amore sighting, but that orchid had turned out to be just a *dichaea muricate*. A common variant.

Their disappointment had been so great that they consoled themselves in each other's arms. It was stupid. They'd had too much to drink, and afterward they'd sworn never to speak of their short-lived affair again, and on the surface, it seemed that their working relationship had gone back to normal.

But now, Dr. Hampton's stubbornness to acknowledge that her theory had merit told Madison she'd been deceiving herself. Hampton wasn't about to admit she was onto something. His ego getting in the way, even to the point of letting it impede the chance to finally fulfill his quest.

Well, fine. If Hampton was with her when she found the amore, he'd take the credit for it anyway. This way, she'd get the accolades.

Whichever, she had to stop ruminating and get some sleep. She had a big day ahead of her. Who knew? Maybe tomorrow her most cherished dream would come true.

MADISON HAD TOLD JAKE to meet her at six because she wanted to leave the camp before Dr. Hampton and his entourage. When she got to the cantina, Jake was already there, stuffing muffins in his backpack and swilling coffee.

No one else was out and about this early.

When he saw her, he pushed his glasses up on his nose and then grinned as if he was truly glad to see her.

Suddenly, her pulse sped up for no good reason.

"Mornin'." He spoke with a drawl and the word felt like a caress.

Heightened awareness shot through her, and she curled her hands into fists. Madison moved ahead of him, feeling the silky lingerie shift sexily over her skin. She shouldn't have worn the damned thing. This was certainly not wilderness attire, but she'd made that silly bet with her friends, and promised Bianca, she'd wear it, so she'd put it on as a reminder of what not to do.

"Let's go."

"Good morning to you too, Jake," he said in a mocking tone. "I hope you slept well."

Ignoring him, she filled her own backpack with food, shouldered it, and headed out of camp. She sensed Jake fall in behind her, but she did not turn her head to look at him.

The eastern sky was tinged purple as they trudged into the darkened jungle. Jake came up beside her, walking abreast, even though the narrow path they were on required walking in single file. Palm fronds brushed against their legs, and their shoulders made contact.

Madison veered away from him, stumbling over a tree root, but she quickly regained her balance. "Why don't you stay behind me?"

"It's more fun being beside you. And it's easier to talk when we're side by side."

"But not easier to walk."

"You—" He bit off whatever else he was going to say.

She glared at him. "What?"

"Nothing."

"Look, I'm not much of a talker. I enjoy peace and quiet. So how about we just not have a peppy early morning conversation."

"You're shutting me down?"

"Look, you're the one who wanted to come with me, not the other way around."

He snickered.

"What?"

"You forbid from saying that word yesterday."

Oh dear Lord, what was he? Thirteen? "I forbid *you* from saying come. I didn't give myself the same restrictions."

"Ahh, so that's how it is."

"That's how it is," she said, realizing she sounded unreasonable and not caring a fig.

"You're the boss. My lips are sealed until you tell me otherwise."

"I just want you to pay attention to the task at hand." She let go of her acrimony. Her pique with Dr. Hampton was not his fault.

"Okay."

"We're entering a tropical rain forest, and the sun isn't even up yet. There're all kinds of wildlife here, some of it is unfriendly to humans. Let's stay on our toes."

"Do you know a lot about Costa Rican wildlife?"

Honestly, nothing more than what she'd read about in the guidebooks. Her entire focus had been on finding the amore orchid, not the physical challenges of the terrain surrounding it.

"Why are you here?" she asked.

He said nothing.

"Seriously, you're not going to talk?"

He grinned, shrugged.

"You may speak now."

He exhaled loudly. "I thought you didn't want conversation."

"Tell the truth. Why are you here? You don't look like any orchid enthusiast I've ever met."

"What makes you say that?"

"For one thing, you're under thirty."

"So?"

"There are very few young heterosexual men who are interested in orchids."

"Who says I'm heterosexual?"

She rolled her eyes. "Your so cis you squeak."

"Stereotyping me?"

She cocked her head and studied him. "Am I?"

"Well, I'm not your ordinary flower guy."

She let it go for the moment, and eventually, he fell back behind her as they traveled deeper into the jungle, allowing her to lead.

Sunlight slowly began filtering in through the lush vegetation, and the sounds of the rain forest were all around them—exotic birds, the scurrying of small animals, the clicking of insects, little howler monkeys warning them off with big voices.

It was a vivid green world filled with life and energy. Madison took a deep breath of the humid air, sweet with the smell of tropical flowers. She wondered what the amore orchid smelled like. Whether it was as sensual and overwhelming as everyone claimed.

As if reading her mind, Jake asked, "Do you think the rumors about the amore are true?"

"What rumors?" She feigned ignorance, then immediately wondered why she'd done that. If she pretended to be clueless about that legend, that meant he'd have to fill her in, and the last thing she wanted was to talk about sex with Jake.

To reverse the challenge, she'd inadvertently instigated, she stopped short, and he almost plowed into her. She remembered last night when she'd plowed into *him* and they'd tumbled to the ground, their bodies entangled.

She heard a rustling in the distance and put out her arm to stop him. "What was that noise?"

"What noise?"

"Um... I don't hear it now."

"What did it sound like?"

"Like a noise." She started walking again.

He rushed to catch up. "When we find this field of amore orchids, are you prepared for the consequences?"

"Consequences?"

"You know, the legend of the amore. One whiff and—"

"What? You think one sniff of the orchid will drive me wild, and I'll rip your clothes off?"

"A guy can hope." His laugh rang out across the jungle landscape.

Red flag number four.

But where that should have ticked her off, instead, she felt flattered. It had been a long time since a guy had flirted this outrageously with her.

"Don't be ridiculous," she said. "No plant can make a person act out of character."

"Meaning you're not the type of woman who would rip off a stranger's clothes and make love to him in a field of orchids even if you were madly attracted to him?"

Honestly, she'd love to have sex surrounded by the amore orchids. It was one of her biggest sexual fantasies, but no way was she going to tell this guy. "I'm not the least bit attracted to you."

"Ha!"

"Ha? What the hell does that mean?"

"You're attracted to me."

"You're full of yourself."

"That doesn't change the fact that you're interested."

"Jeez, the ego on you. Where'd you get it? Egos Are Us?"

"Witty."

"Thank you. Now, could you please stay behind me? You're getting on my last nerve."

"Maybe you should be behind me," he said.

"Why on earth would I do that?"

"Because you're about to walk right off the edge of a cliff."

"I am not—"

But she didn't even get the words out of her mouth. One minute, she was standing on firm ground, the next second, she'd taken a step forward into a thicket of vegetation, and the ground just disappeared from underneath her.

Chapter Three

Madison's scream echoed throughout the jungle.

"Holy cow." The hairs on Jake's nape stood up.

One second, she'd been arguing with him like she knew what she was talking about, and the next, she was sliding headlong down a cliff of tropical vegetation, barreling straight toward a rushing stream several hundred yards below them.

"Maddie, are you okay?" His pulse skittered, out of control. He heard a series of small yelps, but she didn't answer him, and panic gripped his throat. "Hang on, I'm coming for you!"

Oops, she didn't like that word.

"I mean I'm... er... I'll rescue you."

Feeling as though he'd just stepped into *Romancing the Stone* movie set, Jake leaned over to peer down the incline.

The ground crumbled beneath him.

The next thing he knew, Jake was sluicing down the slick, green plant-chute at breakneck speed. And it was more exciting than taming a wild mustang.

Okay, now he knew why she was screaming. It was a damned scary sensation, even for a cowboy who trained cutting horses.

Seconds later, he shot from the muddy flume and landed in chest deep water.

Instantly, he was caught up in a powerful eddy that sent him barreling downstream. He sputtered, and kicked, grabbing for a tree branch to stop himself. Missed once, twice, three times. He spun to the middle of the stream, tried to shove the wet hair from his eyes to see if he could find Madison.

She was bound to be terrified, poor woman.

He opened his mouth to call out to her, but water filled it and he spit. Yuck. Jake fought to swim, but his backpack weighed him down, pulling him under again. He gulped in more nasty jungle water and started coughing.

Get yourself together. Shake it off.

Jake blinked, struggling to get his footing. Then—*ouch!*

Something snatched at his hair. He muttered a colorful curse word as he felt himself being dragged.

Disoriented, he kicked, slapped the surrounding air. Who or what had hold of time?

"Stop it."

Then just like that, he was lying spread-eagle on the ground underneath a guanacaste tree, and Madison was standing over him, looking pissed. Her midnight-black hair was plastered to her face, and her wet clothes clung to her body.

Outlining every curve.

From his position on the ground, the view was fantastic.

Jake enjoyed the way her shirt molded to her breasts, revealing that Maddie was hiding some very nice assets underneath her baggy attire.

How had she gotten out of the water on her own and then turned right around and save his sorry ass?

He was at once admiring and puzzled. There was more to this woman than met the eye.

Jake rolled over onto his side and stayed there, noticing the way her cargo shorts wrapped around her pale thighs. He'd never thought pale was a good color until he saw it on Maddie.

"Get up," she said.

"What are you? A drill sergeant?"

"You're lying in a pack of leeches."

"Leeches!" He yelped and shot to his feet, slapping himself. "I hate leeches. Get 'em off, get 'em off."

Maddie burst out laughing.

He glared at her. "Leeches are not a laughing matter."

"I lied. It's not leeches, just leaves."

He was so relieved that he wasn't even mad. "Why'd you do that?"

"So that you'd stop staring up at me with that goofy expression on your face."

"You do know how to command people."

"Thanks for the compliment."

"Don't get me wrong. That was a complaint." He put his palms to his back and stretched.

"You lost your glasses in the fall," she said.

"Oh, yeah." He squinted intentionally, trying to appear myopic.

She gave him an odd look.

"How did you hang on to yours?" he asked.

"I grabbed hold of them as soon as I tripped. I can't see a thing without them, and I wasn't about to let go."

He didn't want her to pose to him any more glasses-related questions, so he stared up at the cliff that had completely dissolved underneath them.

It was at least the length of two football fields straight up and there was no climbing it.

"Now we have to figure out how to get back on the main trail," he said.

"That does seem to pose a problem." She rested her hands on her hips.

He turned his head to study her. "You're not freaking out."

"Why would I freak out?"

"Most women I've known would."

"Well, you've never known me."

"This is true, but you gotta admit you don't really look like an outdoorsy girl, either. All the pale skin. Just saying."

"I can't help that I'm pale."

"You don't tan?"

"Nope."

"Got vampire lineage?"

She laughed. "I have to wear a gob of sunscreen, or I burn to a crisp."

"Well, whatever it is, it's working for you."

"Why don't we just take that path?" She ignored his compliment.

"What path?"

Madison pointed to a faint trail that disappeared into the jungle beyond. "I'm just praying it doesn't lead to a jaguar's den or something equally terrifying."

"Well?" Jake grinned. "What are we waiting for? Let's get a move on."

THEY'D BEEN HIKING for well over two hours when the rain started.

Not just a little spattering, either. Not sprinkles nor raindrops nor summer showers. This was an honest-to-Pete deluge.

Huge sheets of water poured from a dark sky, drenching them to the skin. At least it washed the mud away.

Madison tried to console herself with logic, but she wasn't up to the challenge. Even though the temperature scorching hot, the abundant, constant rain made her shiver.

Jake looked as miserable as she felt. They stumbled against the onslaught. The ground churned to mud beneath their feet. To make their way, they had to cling to trees and fronds, anything they could grab on to. It was amid this verdant hell that Jake let out a hoot of delight.

For a moment, Madison thought he might have lost his mind. Especially when he started running.

Or rather running, slipping, falling, getting back up, and running again.

She searched the jungle, trying to see where he was going. And then, through the mass of water and the thicket of greenery, she saw it. A little wooden hut balanced on the top of a rise, almost completely hidden by the trees.

The introvert in her worried that someone lived there, and they'd be intruding, but her practical side told her to get over her shyness and follow Jake.

He stopped and turned back to her. "Stay here and let me check this out. It might not be safe."

Madison paused. Costa Rica didn't have political turmoil, but some of the neighboring countries did. What if refugees were huddled in the hut?

Clearly, he'd considered it.

She halted in mid-stride, rain rolling down her face, as she waited while Jake scaled the slippery hill to the hut.

It was a short distance, but the trip took him a long time in the muck and mire. He cut a dashing figure—agile and quick—and her breath caught in her lungs. Oh, yes, he was much more than he seemed.

From the time she was a small kid, she'd been enchanted by stories of swashbucklers and rollicking adventures. She'd cut her teeth on Jules Verne and Edgar Rice Burroughs. She loved *Indiana Jones* and *Romancing the Stone* and *The Lost City*. Or really any movie or book fraught with danger and thrilling quests.

Mainly because she had so little of those elements in her own quiet, bookish life. There might be something not quite right about Jake, but right now, she was just going to enjoy being part of an adventure.

She wondered why she'd let him scramble off without her. She wasn't some helpless flower.

Several minutes after he entered the hut, Jake appeared on the small ledge that barely qualified as a front porch and waved her up.

"C'mon, it's empty and dry inside."

"Good idea." She started up the rise but couldn't find a decent foothold.

How in the world had he climbed this? After several minutes of struggling, a rope suddenly appeared in front of her face. She glanced up to see Jake standing above her, holding the other end of the rope and grinning.

"Grab on and I'll pull you up."

After several minutes of grunting and tugging, Madison hauled herself up over the side of the hill and collapsed onto the ground at his feet, breathing like a landed guppy. She was covered in mud and drenched to her soul, but she'd made it.

"Well done." Jake put down a hand to help her up.

She touched his hand, and there it was again, that same spark, that same strike of electricity. It was so powerful she almost lost her balance and tumbled back down over the ledge. But Jake held on to her, drawing her closer.

"Whoa there, Maddie."

She'd always disliked the nickname. The moniker belonged to a lighthearted person, not a serious scientist. Even when she was quite small, she'd insisted everyone call her Madison, and she got huffy when any of her friends—usually Izzy—dared call her Maddie.

But when Jake said it, the name sounded like cool water trickling over hot rocks. What was it about the guy that so appealed to her? She didn't believe in love at first sight.

Heck, she'd suspected him from the minute she'd laid eyes on him, but there was something about the guy that just pushed all the right sexual buttons inside her and to hell with everything else.

Why?

Don't forget what happened last year when you threw caution to the wind with Hampton. You ended up with regrets. Don't make that same mistake.

She wouldn't.

"Let's get inside," Jake said, pulling her even closer. His breath was warm against her ear, and she allowed him to guide her into the hut.

As domiciles went, it was basic. One room. Roof made of palm fronds. Terra cotta tile floor. A camp stove in one corner. Outhouse in the back. And that was it.

Shelter from the weather and really nothing more. But it was dry and relatively free of creatures, although she did spy a couple of click beetles scuttling across the floor. Not exactly the Ritz, but it would do in a pinch.

"Do you have a change of clothes in that backpack?" he asked.

"Yeah."

"There's an outdoor shower on the back porch," he said. "If you want to rinse the mud off."

She did. "Thanks."

"You can go first," he said, waving his hand in a magnanimous gesture.

Madison went to the porch and saw that the shower was nothing more than a water tower spout. Still, it was something. Of course, she would not get naked. Not with Jake inside the hut. She didn't trust him not to peek out at her. Was that a red flag? She couldn't decide.

"Got a towel?" he asked.

She shook her head. "I didn't think to bring one."

"Don't worry. I've got you covered." He plucked a towel from his own backpack and gave it to her.

The towel smelled of him, sandalwood and cedar. She pressed it to her face, then looked over and saw he was holding out a bar of soap.

"Were you ever a Boy Scout?"

"Why do you ask?"

"You seem prepared for everything."

His grin widened. "Nope, no Boy Scout here. I told you, I know my way around the wilderness."

"A regular Tarzan, huh?"

He pounded on his chest with his fists and made Tarzan noises.

"Okay, that was cringy," Madison said.

"Didn't do much for my sex appeal?" He wriggled his eyebrows.

"Negative four on a scale of one to ten."

"No more chest pounding. Got it." He grinned.

She was struck again by the paradox of this man. Who was he really? Orchid nerd, or something else entirely?

She couldn't help smiling back, though, as she headed for the porch, soap in hand. She left the towel inside on a hook at the door and stepped out into the rain. It seemed dumb to shower in a deluge, but she felt grimy, and stripped out of her clothes—save for the sexy underwear—and cast a glance over her shoulder to see if Jake was peering at her from the door.

To her disappointment, he was not.

Why are you disappointed? Thank heavens he's not a voyeur.

She turned and busied with the shower, reminding herself that despite the sparks between them, she knew absolutely nothing about this man.

JAKE SAUNTERED OVER to the far of the hut, trying to give Madison as much privacy as he could. But discovered to his alarm that he could see her reflection in the windowpane. From this vantage point, he could see her, but Maddie wouldn't be able to see him.

He watched her shimmy out of her clothes, and his heart jack hammered. *Okay, not cool, Strickland. No staring.*

But he couldn't seem to help himself.

Maddie had a body worth ogling. She didn't get all the way naked, and somehow that was even sexier than total nudity. She wore a skimpy little pink-and-white matching bra and panties with some little belt thing that connected the two at the waist.

And what a body!

It was even better than he'd imagine. Why did she hide herself beneath those baggy clothes?

Jake felt himself harden. *Hold up, fella. She's certainly not on the menu. Especially when you're planning on stealing those orchids out from under her.*

Still, he realized he was feeling more than simple lust. This was extreme interest combined with intense curiosity and a strange bone-deep yearning. Whenever he looked at her, he experienced a strange tingling in his chest.

What was it about her that so intrigued him? Was it her intelligence? Her sharp wit? The way she didn't put up with his baloney?

There might be something to that last part. He was used to women draping themselves all over him. Madison acted as though he wasn't worth her time.

Cowboy, this is so messed up. You want a woman who's not into you.

He couldn't remember ever being interested in a woman who had no interest in him. Women were *always* interested in him. He stepped away from the window, feeling ashamed of himself.

She was getting to him. His feelings were bizarre, surreal. It was like... fate.

Don't be a putz. You don't even know her, and she doesn't know you. She'd hate you if she knew.

And yet, he couldn't stop thinking about her.

He imagined her touching him. A phantom caress that electrified every nerve ending in his body. He visualized her long dark hair lightly tickling his bare skin. He could taste her on his tongue—warm, feminine, alive.

Jake shoved a hand through his hair, hauling in a deep breath. A strange panic settled all the way into his bones.

What in the hell was this feeling?

Better question, how could he make it go away.

Chapter Four

Madison poked her head through the door and grabbed the towel off the hook. "Turn around."

"Huh?"

"Turn your back. I don't want you to see me."

"Fine." Sighing, Jake spun around.

Madison slipped inside the room and wrapped the bath towel around her. The sexy underwear was plastered to her skin.

Quickly, she whisked the towel over her body, getting as dry as she could, then tied her wet hair up with the towel, tucking it into a turban. After that, she tiptoed across the floor to her backpack.

"Keep looking at the wall."

"I saw your reflection in the windowpane. I didn't mean to stare but I did, and I'm sorry."

"Are you?"

"I'm sorry I violated your privacy, but I'm not really sorry I saw you."

"Darn it."

The air felt charged. Jake was still staring at the wall and she got a great view of his butt. How could she blame him for ogling her when all she wanted to do was ogle him?

"What are you so afraid of, Maddie?"

"You."

"Why?"

"I don't even know you. You could be a perv."

"I'm not."

"Would you admit it if you were one?"

"I suppose not." He paused.

Silence consumed the hut. Madison was fine with quiet.

"Will you tell me just one thing?" he asked.

"No."

"Are those undies you're wearing what I think it is?"

"What do you think it is?"

"Lingerie for sex play? It looks like there's a GPS sensor in the bodice."

"How do you know that?"

"I once had this girlfriend who liked to play hide and seek—"

"I don't really need the blow-by-blow details of your love life, thank you very much."

"You asked."

"Sorry, my mistake."

Madison yanked her spare pair of jeans from her backpack and wriggled into them. Then she fished out a white oversize T-shirt and pulled that on as well, being careful not to knock the towel off her head.

"Okay, you can turn around," she said.

Jake pivoted to face her, that ubiquitous grin on his face. Did the man ever stop smiling? "Why do you wear clothes that are too big for you when you have such a smoking hot body?"

"Maybe so assholes such as yourself don't leer at me."

"Hey, I haven't given you any reason to call me names."

"You're too cocky."

"Why don't you like me?"

She shrugged. "I know your type. You breeze through life on your own terms, not caring who you hurt in the process."

"Are you talking about Dr. Hampton?" Jake asked. "Because if feels like you've got a chip on your shoulder. Did you two have a fling that went bad?"

Madison wrinkled her nose. "No. Yes. Maybe. Sort of."

"Which is it?"

"It's not just Hampton."

"No?"

"I have a tendency to fall for the ne'er-do-wells."

"Ne'er-do-wells?" Jake laughed. "Who are you? Jane Austen?"

Madison went on the defensive. "What's wrong with Jane Austen? She's my favorite writer."

"There's nothing wrong with Jane Austen if you're Jane Austen. You, however, are Maddie Garrett."

"Madison," she corrected.

"Tell me about the ne'er-do-wells."

"Why?"

He waved a hand at the rain slanting hard in front of the hut. "Not much else to do."

"Besides Hampton?"

"Besides him. How many were there?"

"That's a personal question. I'm not telling you my number."

He shrugged.

"Four ne're-do-wells," she said, not knowing why she admitted that to him. "Five if you count my father. He was the guy who'd promised you the sky, then disappeared on your sixth birthday and would only show up every couple of years to take you to Coney Island, assuming that would make up for everything."

"Ouch. I'm sorry."

She shrugged. "I'm over it."

"Are you really?"

"Yes," she said.

She had gotten over anger at her father. In fact, she'd forgiven him, and she saw him more often now than she had when she was a kid. But she still feared she was susceptible to good-looking, dark-haired men with winsome smiles.

"And the second one?"

"High school sweetheart. The usual story. Captain of the football team. Couldn't believe he was interested in me. Caught him with the head cheerleader. Learned he was dating me just to get me to do his homework."

"And the third?"

"Fiancé."

"Left you at the altar?"

"No, I left *him* after I realized I was trying to tame a man who couldn't be tamed."

"A twist. I like it."

"I'm not looking for your approval."

"No?"

"Not in the least."

"The fourth?" he prodded.

"Hampton. Short-term fling. Rebound from the fiancé."

Jake shrugged. "Good enough for me. I guess it's my turn at the shower." He held out his hand.

"What?"

"My soap and towel. Could I have them back?"

"Oh. Yeah." She found the soap she'd left sitting on her bag, unwound his towel from around her hair, and gave both items to him. "I'm afraid the towel is pretty wet."

He raked an unholy gaze over her. "Wet's okay with me."

After he'd disappeared out the door, Madison paced the empty hut. Why was she so edgy? So itchy? So…

What?

What was she feeling? Why was she so attracted to a guy she didn't even know? It was beyond all logic, and Madison was logical if nothing else.

What was this unexpected chemistry between herself and Strickland? And most important of all, why was she letting it get to her?

Whenever she looked at him, her mind just went haywire, and all she could do was imagine him naked. Her heart would start hammering, and her nipples would harden, and her womb would contract.

In despair, she stared out the window at the driving rain and wondered just how long they would be stuck here. If it didn't stop raining soon, Madison was terrified that she'd fall for one more ne'er-do-well.

"YOU HUNGRY?" JAKE ASKED, toweling his hair dry after he got out of the shower.

"Starved. What did you bring with you?"

"Protein bars, trail mix, bananas, peanut butter and a handful of muffins from the breakfast buffet. You?"

"I've got string cheese, turkey jerky, and dehydrated soup mix. Big package of peanuts and two apples," she said.

"We've got the makings of a picnic." Jake plunked down on the floor of the hut.

Madison sat down beside him. They went through their waterproof backpacks and came up with the food, spreading it out in front of them.

"So," she said, peeling a banana. "I told you about my ne'er-do-wells. What's your story? You married?"

He raised his left hand, bare of any rings. "Footloose and fancy-free."

She hadn't thought he was married, but she wanted it confirmed. Not that she really cared. "Ever been married?"

"Not even close."

"How old are you?" She unpeeled a banana.

"Twenty-nine."

"Peter Pan complex?"

"Nah, just not all that impressed with the institution of marriage."

"You come from a broken home, too?"

"Fractured is more like it. I never knew my dad. My mom... well, let's just say she's a real peach. She married a guy who didn't want children, so she left me with my grandmother, who died shortly after I went to live with her. That's when I learned the joys of the foster care system."

Sympathy tugged at her heart. "Oh, Jake. How old were you?"

"Seven."

"Poor kid." She had an urge to reach out and hug him, and Madison was not the huggy type.

He mugged a mournful face. "It is tough being me."

"I wasn't making fun."

"I know. I was."

"I can't imagine what that must have been like for you. And here I was whining because I had a jack-in-the-box dad who showed up when I least expected it. At least he did eventually show up."

"Hey, don't feel sorry for me. I ran away when I was twelve, and I met this great guy, Deke Maxwell. He took me in, gave me a job mucking out stalls on his ranch, and treated me as if I were his son."

"Deke sounds like an honorable man."

"He is." Jake nodded.

"What about school?"

"Not so great at academics, but I shone on the track field."

"I bet you were popular with the girls."

He looked surprised. "How did you guess?"

"With that face? Come on."

"You think I'm handsome?"

"I think you're a man who knows exactly the effect he has on the opposite sex."

"So, you admit I affect you," he said, nibbling on a handful of trail mix.

Madison couldn't stop watching the column of his throat move when he swallowed, couldn't stop her eyes from sliding down to where the *V* of his shirt revealed a sexy sprinkling of chest hairs.

"Hell no." She lied through her teeth.

"Whew." He dragged a hand across his forehead, wiping off imaginary sweat.

"Whew? You're relieved I'm not attracted to you?"

"Yeah."

"Why is that?" she asked, knowing she shouldn't, but her old insecurities welled up. With men, she was so inept. Falling for the wrong ones, not falling for the right ones. It was best if she just stayed away.

"Because if you were as attracted to me as I am attracted to you, we'd spontaneously combust."

Oh dammit, why had he said that? And why was he staring at her as if she was the most fascinating woman on the face of the earth?

"You're a ne'er-do-well in nerd's clothing and I have to ask myself why?"

"That's where you're wrong," he said.

"What about?"

He cocked an eyebrow, blatantly studying her lips. "There are a lot of things I do very well."

Don't fall for it. Don't you dare fall for it. Seriously, stop looking at him. Stop thinking about him. Calm down. Cool down.

Just then, her satellite phone rang. She had to dig to the bottom of her backpack for it. Saved by the ring tone.

"Madison? It's Izzy, are you okay?"

"Sure," Madison said. "Why wouldn't I be okay?"

"You sound off. Are you overexerting yourself in the jungle?"

Madison glanced over at Jake, who cracked one of those *do me, darlin'* grins of his, and she glanced away. "We... um... I got lost."

"We?"

"*I'm* fine."

"You sound weird. Did guerillas take you hostage?"

"Costa Rica is perfectly safe."

"Why is your voice... Omigosh, you're with a guy! That's why you said 'we.'"

"I'm in a stressful situation, Izzy. I really don't have time for a phone call."

"Is he cute? I bet he's cute."

"I'm going to hang up now."

"So, you're out of the bet?"

"Is that why you called? No, I'm not out of the bet."

"Rats," Izzy said.

"You're my friend. You should be helping me stay celibate."

"You're nuts. I'm out to win five hundred dollars."

"Izzy!"

"Okay, okay, listen to me, Madison. You will not have sex with this guy."

"Of course not."

"But you want to." Izzy laughed.

"I do not!"

"I beg to differ. The stress in your voice says otherwise. And here everyone thought you were the one who'd win our wager."

"I'm not having sex," Madison said in a tense tone.

"Ooh, you get cranky when you're not getting any." Izzy laughed.

Madison notched her chin upward. "I *am* going to win the bet."

She could feel the heat of Jake's gaze on her, but she refused to look up at him. "I've got it under control."

"You sure about that?"

"Absolutely."

"All right, but if you sleep with him—"

"I'm not sleeping with him!" she snapped and closed her eyes and let out a soft groan. He'd heard that.

"I believe you."

Madison hung up without even saying goodbye. Sometimes Izzy got on her last nerve. Good thing she loved her friend like a sister. She stuffed the phone back in her bag.

"What was that all about?" Jake asked.

"Long story."

"We got time. And no place to go."

She might as well tell him. He'd already seen her sexy lingerie. "My friends and I have a bet going. An entire summer of no sex."

"What?"

"You heard me."

"Let me guess, does this have something to do with that sexy underwear you're wearing."

"Yeah," she admitted.

"Is this like that episode of *Seinfeld* where Jerry and George and Kramer and Elaine all vow not to, um... have any kind of sexual contact?"

"It's exactly like that."

"Better you than me." Jake shook his head.

"Are you saying you have no self-control?"

"Depends. How much is the wager?"

"Five hundred dollars."

"No way. It would take a lot more cash to keep me from pursuing a woman I was interested in." He eyed her.

"How much would it take?"

He shrugged. "I dunno."

"Put a price on it. How much would it take to keep you celibate?"

"With a woman like you?" His grin turned downright sinful. "Million and a half."

Her pulse quickened. "Why the half?"

"Taxes."

Madison laughed. She didn't even know why. But the way Jake was looking at her made her feel desired and wanted in a way she'd never quite felt before.

"Listen, I like you. A lot. And I'm feeling things. Lots of things. But this bet is important to me. I can't let myself get involved with you."

"You want me to go outside?"

"No, just stop staring at me and talk about something boring."

"Boring, huh?"

"Really boring. Your last dental appointment might work."

"That would cool off anyone," he said. "I had two cavities the last time."

"Sweet tooth?"

"You got it." He winked, and she felt a blush heat her cheeks. Dammit. She'd never get herself under control at this rate.

"All right, that's not working. I need to calm down. There's been too much excitement for one day."

"Wanna try yoga breathwork?" he asked.

"You know about that?"

"Sure."

She eyed him. That was a surprise. "Okay, what do I need to do?"

"Breathe from deep in your diaphragm." He placed a palm on his belly and inhaled deeply.

Madison followed suit, and they breathed together quickly, and she felt her body relax. It was working.

"Close your eyes."

She did.

"Put your index fingers to your thumbs and make a circle."

She did that as well.

"Now, just keep breathing like that."

In a few minutes, a gentle peace had settled over her. Crisis averted. She opened her eyes and found Jake's eyes on her. "What are you looking at?"

"You've got a little banana right there." He touched his own face just above his upper lip.

"Where?" She rubbed her face with her fingers.

"Missed it."

She swiped her whole palm over her mouth. "How about now?"

"Still there."

She scrubbed her face. "That get it?"

"No." He leaned in toward her and softly brushed his index finger over the spot. His touch sent tingles racing through her body.

Their gazes locked.

He was so close to her she could feel the heat of his breath on her skin. Goose bumps carpeted her arms. They stared at each other. The calmness evaporated.

Madison couldn't say who made the first move. She thought it was him, but it certainly could have been her.

Most likely it was both of them simultaneously riding the wave of attraction and going for it, but the next thing she knew, Jake's mouth was on hers, and hers was on his, and her wet hair was tumbling to her shoulders, and his hot arms were encircling her, and they were kissing like there was no tomorrow.

Chapter Five

Jake sure as hell hadn't meant to kiss her. He'd been trying not to kiss her the entire day. One minute he was telling himself, *don't kiss her, don't you dare kiss her,* and the next minute he had her in a lip-lock so startlingly delicious he forgot to breathe.

All he could do was inhale.

Maddie, he thought. *Maddie, Maddie, Maddie.*

He tightened his arms around her waist, and she linked her arms around his neck, and they were on the ground, Maddie's soft breasts mashed beneath his hard chest muscles. She tasted like peach nectar, thick and sweet and heavenly.

He kissed her as if his very life depended on it. Kissed and kissed and kissed *and...*

Then her damned cell phone rang.

Her friend again, he wondered, calling her out to see if she was having sex?

Well, not quite sex. Not yet. But they were well on their way.

Instantly, Jake broke off the kiss and rolled off her, his head spinning. Somewhere along the way, he'd unbuttoned Maddie's jeans. Hell, he didn't even remember doing that. What was happening to him? He felt shaky and breathless.

Unless she'd undone the jeans herself.

This is crazy. You can't be falling for her. No way, no how. Wrong time, wrong place, wrong woman, wrong everything.

And yet, one look into her eyes and he was helpless. She could ask him whatever she wanted, and he'd give it to her.

This was crazy. Nonsensical. And he didn't like it one damn bit.

Madison scrambled for her phone, and she was assuring a different friend, this one called Bianca, that she was not having sex. It wasn't a total lie, because they'd been rushing headlong toward it.

He got up, paced to the door, shoved a hand through his hair, and stared out at the downpour. Good grief, they were trapped here until it stopped raining.

Jake scanned the sky, which seemed to grow darker and wetter with each passing moment and her tried to ignore the ache in his rock-hard shaft. He could smell Maddie on his skin, taste her on his lips. She was an amazing woman.

If they weren't in Costa Rica and she wasn't a conservationist and he wasn't an orchid smuggler, well... But he *was* an orchid smuggler, and she was a conservationist, and even beyond that was the whole footloose and fancy-free motto that defined him.

He wasn't changing for any woman, even one as compelling as this one. Even though whenever he looked at her, he felt something click inside him as if, for the first time, everything was right with the world.

"Are you okay?" Maddie asked, coming up behind him.

Jake blinked, glancing over his shoulder at her.

She was off the phone.

"I'm fine," he said.

"You don't look fine."

"Well, I am fine."

She squared her shoulders. "I'm fine, too."

"Good."

"Great."

"Fine."

"Fine."

"You still going to win your bet?" He nodded at the phone. "You haven't quite crossed a line yet?"

"No," she said, "and I'm not going to."

"That's good. You probably really need those five hundred dollars."

"Not as much as I need my sanity."

They looked at each other, and he could see in her eyes she was as unnerved as he was. He blew out his breath, then said what he'd dreaded telling her.

"It looks like we're going to be stuck here all night or even longer. It's the rainy season in Costa Rica and sometimes it rains for days without letup."

"We need to find something to keep us busy."

He stared at her mouth.

"Not *that*." She brought two fingers to her bottom lip.

Jake stifled a groan. "We need to distract ourselves."

"Do you play cards?" she asked. "I have a deck with me."

"I wouldn't have pegged you for a game player."

"Why not? I *am* a nerd."

"The guys I play poker with at the ran—" Jake broke off, remembering he was supposed to be a botany nerd, not a horse trainer. He floundered for the right venue. "Arboretum. They are cutthroat card players."

Maddie gave him a speculative stare. Did she suspect something? "You play poker?"

"Texas Hold 'Em, mostly."

"We don't have chips for poker. What'll we use?"

He eyed her.

"No strip poker!"

"Agreed."

"I'm glad we agree on something."

"Because that would just be playing with fire."

She glanced away. "How about Gin Rummy? You know how to play that?"

"It's been a while."

Maddie went to her bag and pulled out a deck of cards, then moved to the center of the hut, where she plunked down cross-legged, and started shuffling the cards. Her fingers were long and graceful, and Jake watched, mesmerized.

She looked up, caught his gaze and her breath.

He realized he was holding his breath, too.

They exhaled in unison.

"Well," she said, and dealt the cards. "Here we go."

He wondered if her words held a double meaning. Unless he was deluding himself—which was a distinct possibility—her eyes brimmed with desire.

For *him.*

His gut squeezed and his hands curled into fists of their own accord. It had been a long time since he'd felt this level of interest and heat for a potential partner.

Stop kidding yourself. No matter how hot you are for each other, the second she finds out why you're in Costa Rica, your goose is cooked.

By nature, he was a practical guy. He would do nothing stupid, such as make love to Madison, no matter how much her sweet figure turned him on. Bad idea any way you sliced it.

"You go first," she said.

"Huh?"

"The game. You go first."

"Oh, yeah, right." Jake discarded the ace of clubs.

She scooped it up.

Outside, the rain intensified, and the sky grew so dark it blotted out the sunshine. Jake squinted at his cards. He didn't give two figs about the game. There was a game of a different sort in the forefront of his mind.

They played a few rounds that mostly comprised him discarding and her snatching up his cards.

"You don't strike me as a person who plays frivolous games."

"What?" She slid him a sideways glance. "I can't be complex?"

"Oh, you are extremely complex."

She beamed.

Ahh. He'd found her Achille's heel. She took great pride in her intelligence. Maybe he could use her weakness to his advantage at some point.

"Gin." She fanned out her cards.

"What? Already?"

"You didn't pay close attention and made some dumb moves."

Honestly, he couldn't care less about the card game. What he did care about was getting to know Madison better. She flat out intrigued him. He wasn't accustomed to women like her. He was more used to active, athletic cowgirls.

"Where'd you learn to play cards like that?"

"When I was growing up, my mother's father was a statistician for MIT." She shuffled again for a new hand. "Granddad played all kinds of math games with us kids. Including cards."

"No kidding. Is he still around?"

"Yes, seventy-three and going strong."

"What does he do now?"

"He builds bridges in third world countries."

"So, he's a diplomat?"

"No, he literally builds bridges."

"Really? That's so interesting."

"He works for a nonprofit."

"What about your mom? What does she do?"

"Mom's a tenured Harvard professor."

"Wow." Jake was impressed. She was so far out of his league it hurt, but knowing that only stoked his interest in her, rather than dampening it.

"What about you?" She discarded a ten of hearts. "What do your parents do?"

Jack picked up and slid it into the run of hearts that he was collecting. "I grew up in foster homes."

She made a soft sound of distress. "Oh, I'm so sorry."

"Don't be. I made peace with it a long time ago, and I have a really great surrogate father. I've learned it's not where you start in life that matters, but where you finish."

"What a terrific attitude." She gifted him with a brilliant smile that warmed him from the inside out.

Lightning flashed, quickly followed by hard thunder. Madison jumped.

"Are you okay?" he asked.

"Thunderstorms make me nervous. Our house got hit by lightning when I was a kid and it burned to the ground."

"That must have been traumatic."

She shrugged, but he could see the anxiety in her eyes. "It's no biggie. I just get antsy during thunderstorms."

"What helps you relax?"

"I normally wrap myself up tight in a blanket and play soothing music."

"If you'd like a comforting hug, I've been told I give pretty good ones." Inwardly, Jake winced. Had he sounded like a creep? "Strictly a therapeutic hug. I'm not trying anything hinky."

The lightning and thunder did its thing again, and Madison shivered.

Jake opened his arms, just to let her know she was welcomed there, but the speed with which she tossed her cards aside and launched herself into his arms surprised him.

Okay, then. This was nice. Smiling over her head, Jake pulled her close and held Madison tight as the storm raged on.

She rested her head on his shoulder and he could feel the crazy tempo of her pulse beating at her throat. He tightened his arms around her, and they sat there for the longest time listen to the storm slowly pass.

And dang if he didn't feel a gentle swell of some tender emotion, he didn't understand or have a name for, as it grew right underneath his ribcage.

In a very short time, Madison had altered his outlook on possibilities, but as the guilt crept in, he realized by coming here to steal orchids, he'd sown himself into a pouch so tight, he had no way of getting out of this adventure with either his self-image, or his heart, intact.

MADISON FINALLY CAME to her senses and eased herself from Jake's comforting embrace.

He let her go easily. Not clinging, but he did put a hand to her elbow to steady her as she got to her feet.

A hand so hot it seemed to burn her tender skin.

"I... um... gotta go... um..." She gestured toward door. "Outhouse."

She ducked her head so he couldn't see her eyes. Eye contact seemed way too intense right now. She needed some space from him, but the thought of going out into the rain—even if the thunder and lightning had passed—was daunting.

She bit her bottom lip, feeling achy and restless, the sexual tension seeping into her bones. She needed to get away, get some perspective on her emotions, but there was nowhere to go.

Trapped.

Madison was stranded with the sexiest man she'd ever met, and her body was waging an all-out war with her mind. She rushed outside and shut the door behind her, standing on the little awning over the hut, noticing the thick green canopy of trees glistening as sunlight peeped through an opening in the clouds and reflected off the raindrops.

The jungle bathed in a magical, mystical glow.

It felt like some kind of sign.

Not that she believed in stuff like that, but her heart was racing, and she had no reason for it. She felt both panicky and elated, her entire body tingling from toe to scalp.

She leaned over to peek into the window and there stood Jake in the middle of the hut, bathed in the same sunlight that lit her up.

His eyes met hers through the rain slick pane.

Bam! Sweet punch to the gut.

She'd never felt such potent chemistry with a man, and it was disconcerting. Quickly, she jerked back and willed her knees to stop wobbling.

Bracing her palm against a wet tree trunk to steady her, Madison slowly picked her way up a muddy path leading to the outhouse she'd spotted when she was in the outdoor shower. Her shirt sticking against her spine.

By the time she finished up in the outhouse, the sun had disappeared, and the rain was back in full force. She moved as quickly as dared, fearful about slipping on the muddy path and sliding all the way down the hill to the jungle floor. That thought kept her as surefooted as a mountain goat.

She popped back into the hut to find Jake waiting for her with a dry towel.

"Where'd you get this?" she asked.

"I did a little exploring. There's a storage closet with a few essentials. Even found some toilet paper," he said, settled the towel over her shoulders.

"I sure could have used that five minutes ago. What else didja find?"

"An unopened jug of drinking water, an unrighteous number of Beanie Weenie pull-top cans, a flashlight and batteries, a fireplace lighter, Sterno, and…"

"And?"

"The makings for s'mores."

Their gazes met, and they broke out grinning.

TEN MINUTES LATER, they were eating camp stove s'mores, laughing as melted chocolate and gooey marshmallows stuck to their faces. Watching Madison enjoy the sweet treat tickled Jake's fancy.

Her provocative pink tongue flicked out to lick away the chocolate on her upper lip and Jake's body instantly responded, sending a flush of heat throughout his system. He couldn't take his eyes off her.

She saw he was watching her and put up a hand to cover her mouth. "Oops, I got it all over me."

They were sitting side by side in front of the camp stove, the s'mores paraphernalia on the floor beside them. Jake leaned in closer.

Madison caught her breath. "What are you doing?"

"What does it look like?"

"Are you trying to kiss me?"

"Would you be upset if I did? Cause I don't want you to lose any bets."

She paused a moment, then slowly shook her head. "I wouldn't mind."

That's all he needed to hear. Jake took her into his arms and kissed the sweet mouth he'd been acting to kiss from the moment he'd met her. He'd told himself he could be with her. A relationship with Madison was impossible. They had no future together, but he had a feeling he'd regret it for the rest of his life if he didn't kiss her again.

Her lips parted, and she leaned into him just as hard as he was leaning into her. Moaning, she sank against his chest and he swallowed up her soft sound and the sweet, chocolaty taste of s'mores.

Jake explored her mouth with equal parts lust and awe. Kissing her roused something long dormant in him, an effervescent happiness he hadn't felt in such a long time.

What was going on?

She entangled her fingers in his thick thatch of hair, clearly enjoying this as much as Jake was. Her lips told him through her kisses that she was fully on board.

"Madison." He said her name soft and low, overcome by a sudden tightness in his throat... and in his heart. "*Maddie*."

She didn't correct him.

In fact, she cupped his jaw and planted hot kisses there. Her scent, like the pages of old books mingled with pressed roses, filled his nose pleasurably. He could smell this aroma forever and never grow tired of it.

He stroked his tongue over her lips, and things started to escalate. He pushed past her teeth, fully exploring her warm interior. What a delicious flavor.

His body grew hard. There was no hiding how much he wanted her. Her palms captured both sides of his face and she held him in place as she kissed and kissed and kissed...

"We gotta..." Why did he sound so breathless? "Stop."

"What if I don't want to?"

"Madison, this is... we are..."

"Yes?" She squinted at him. She'd taken off her glasses when they'd started kissing.

"This can't go anywhere."

"Why not?"

"You made that no-sex bet with your friends and I intend on helping you keep it."

"What if I don't care?"

"Your thinking is clouded right now. We shouldn't rush into anything."

She wriggled away from him, her shoulders sagging, her lips moist from his kisses. "What if I wanted to throw caution to the jungle rains?"

"You would regret."

"How can you be so sure?"

Because I'm here to steal your orchid. "Trust me," he said. "I know what I'm talking about."

"You're not married, are you?"

"I am not."

"Then what's the problem? We both love orchids and—"

"You're not a rash person. It's easy to tell. Don't let a little sexual attraction ruin everything you've worked for."

One side of her lip twitched, and she gave a hard shake of her head. "You're right. I lost my head."

"We hardly know each other." He was talking her out of having sex with him when he wanted nothing more than to spend the evening in her arms.

"But this attraction has to mean *something*. Right?" she asked.

"It's just chemistry. Being a botanist, you ought to know all about that."

"Which translates into a great time in bed." She brought her knees to her chest and hugged them, turning her body into a protective shell.

"What if a good time in bed wasn't enough for me?"

She looked startled. "W-what are you saying?"

"I'm saying it's a shame."

"What's a shame?"

"I think you and I could have had something pretty special. Another time, another place."

And that's when a fresh round of thunder and lightning began.

Chapter Six

I think you and I could have had something pretty special.

What had Jake meant? They *could* have had something special. As if they'd miss the boat. As if they'd lost their shot at something meaningful.

Madison's anxiety worried the words around in her head over and over as she lay on her back, staring up at the ceiling and listening to rain drumming on the roof and the soft sound of Jake's easy breathing as they slept side by side.

She should never have kissed him.

That was the problem. As long as she hadn't known what she was missing, everything was okay. By now that she knew what his mouth tasted like, she couldn't shake the cravings. Couldn't shed the fantasies.

In the dim light from her wristwatch, she rolled onto to her side, propping herself up on her elbow and gazing down at the sleeping man beside her.

If her friends could see her now! They'd probably say she was out of the no-sex bet even though she and Jake hadn't gone all the way. They kissed—passionately, and technically, they were sleeping together.

Her body tingled, alive with urgency. More than anything in the world, she ached to lean over and kiss him full on the lips. She admired the way his hair curled at his temple and the strength of his profile. He was so masculine, so far removed from any of the scientists she'd ever known. He was earthy and full-bodied, like a Napa Valley cabernet.

What were these feelings they shared?

It was lust, to be sure, but her feelings ran deeper than that. A powerful undercurrent of something more. Potential.

She'd kept her emotions in check for so long, she had trouble identifying what they were. Her studious mind wouldn't leave it alone. She was desperate to find out what it all meant.

Nothing.

It means absolutely nothing. Yes, he's hot. Yes, you want to jump his bones. Yes, he said there could have been something special. But so what? In the grand scheme of her life, Jake Strickland had no place with her.

Dear heavens, why had she let him kiss her in the first place? It had spoiled everything. Because now, she could think of nothing but him.

She tried to call up the amore orchid in her mind, but it came up fuzzy and unfocused. The only thing clear in her head were images of Jake.

That's when she understood just how much trouble she was in.

IT RAINED FOR TWO SOLID days.

Via her satellite phone, Madison checked in with Dr. Hampton and learned the rest of the group had never left camp because of the inclement weather.

Dammit, why hadn't she checked the forecast? She and Jake were stranded in the jungle all alone and they'd already eaten all the s'mores.

To keep their hands off each other, they'd spent the time talking about their childhoods, their pasts, their likes, and dislikes. They'd played twenty questions and truth or dare, and when they tired of that, they resorted to the childhood game; I spy.

I spy with my little eye, something very sexy, Madison thought as she looked at Jake.

They rationed the food in their backpacks. They shared, splitting everything evenly, and it was enough.

She told him about orchids, why she loved them so much, why she'd spent her life collecting them—moth orchids and lady slippers and Vanda and Cattleya and Burana Sunshine.

Jake couldn't seem to get enough of botany and kept encouraging her to talk. Finally, she got him to admit his favorite thing, and she was surprised to find it was horses. The more he talked about the animals, the more she wondered why he was in Costa Rica and not a rodeo arena. He struck her as much for the cowboy type as a flower nerd.

Then again, she'd always had a thing for cowboys. Maybe she was just trying to get him to fulfill her fantasies.

Through their long talks, they discovered they had much more in common than they would have ever suspected, given their divergent backgrounds. Madison was working on her PhD, and Jake had gotten a GED instead of finishing high school. She was scientific and analytical, while he trusted his gut and acted on instinct. She liked time to think things through; he was fast-paced and action-oriented.

But they both loved rollercoasters and horseback riding. Both were night owls, preferring to sleep in and stay up late. They agreed that while it was noble to be politically active, neither of them had ever bothered to vote. Their favorite comfort food was macaroni and cheese—the kind that came in a box. They preferred the same brand of beer, chose corn chips over potato chips, and thought kettle corn was just plain weird. They learned they shared an obsession with reality TV, and they enjoyed old *B* monster movies. They'd each been to the International Spy Museum in Washington, D.C. and realized to their surprise that they'd both been there on the same day. It felt like a sign.

By the time the rain stopped on the third day, it was as if they'd known each other their entire lives.

They woke from their sleeping bags to the sound of birds chirping and sun flooding in through the boards of the hut. Jake yawned and stretched as Madison put on her glasses and finger-combed her hair.

"Ten o'clock." She strapped on her wristwatch and yawned. "How late did we stay up last night?"

Jake shrugged. "I'm not one for keeping to a schedule, but I think it was pretty late. I was having a lot of fun trying to guess where your birthmark is."

Madison rolled her eyes. She should never have told him about the heart-shaped birthmark. When she'd refused to show it to him, he'd started trying to guess where it was.

"Breasts? Belly? Thigh? Tushy?"

That little game had heated her up quick as his gaze had caressed every part of her body as he called it out.

Remembering, she raised her head and saw Jake giving her the once-over.

Was he remembering, too? A hot rush of sensation passed through her, and she quickly ducked her head.

"You're a beauty, Maddie, even if you don't know it."

Where had that come from?

Madison caught his gaze and cleared her throat. She wasn't accustomed to men complimenting her looks. Her expertise, yes. For her intelligence, sometimes.

Brainy girls, she'd discovered, intimidated most guys. Even the brainy guys because they feared the competition.

But not Jake. Jake seemed genuinely impressed with her.

"We better get a move on," she said. "Today might just be the day we find the amore."

They packed up and started out. The muddy traipse through the jungle quickly grew hot, sweaty, and tiresome, and they were down to their last canteen of water.

Madison kept checking the map and her coordinates. They were so near the amore; she could taste it.

But when they reached the area where she'd calculated that the flowers would be—where the soil nutrients and the rain levels and the amount of sunshine was perfect for orchid growing—there was nothing but more jungle fronds and tall dark trees and mud, mud, mud.

Disappointment swept through her like a snowstorm dusting across the plains. Hampton had been right, and she'd been wrong.

Amore wasn't here.

"Dammit." She startled, realizing she was very near tears.

Madison didn't cry. It took a lot to make her weep. But she'd been so sure...so certain that this spot was it. She'd been passionate about orchids for most of her life, and the amore had captured her imagination. What was she going to do about her dissertation now?

"Madison?"

She didn't answer him, her mind was too wrapped up in her failure. She only had one option. Go back to Hampton with her tail between her legs and beg his forgiveness.

"What's wrong?" Jake asked as they stood in the jungle clearing, staring at the foliage.

She shook her head. "This is where the amore was supposed to be. I was convinced it was here."

"Don't give up hope. The flower is elusive. That doesn't mean it's not here. It could just be hiding from us."

"That's a sweet thing to say, but it's time we headed back. We can't wander aimlessly in the jungle forever. We're almost out of food and water."

"Maybe just a little longer? What would it hurt?"

She looked into his eyes and saw so much belief in her and encouragement that she hardly dared trust it. For so long, she'd wanted a partner who always had her back, and here it seemed as if she'd found one.

Too much, too soon, she warned herself. *You're letting a little flirtation go to your head.*

She wanted to resist his charms, but then he grinned at her and slanted her such a sexy look that it took her breath away.

Oh dear heavens, she was in way too deep and she did not know how it would feel when her high-flying daydreams crashed on solid ground.

JAKE SCRATCHED HIS head and watched Madison stare disappointedly at the trees. Had he bet on the wrong pony? Had he let his attraction to Madison sway his decision to throw in his lot with her instead of sticking with Professor Hampton?

Yeah, probably.

But oddly enough, he didn't really care. Yes, he still wanted to save the ranch, but these last few days with Madison had been among the best in his life. Even without ever having had sex. Maybe precisely because they hadn't had sex.

He'd gotten to know her. A first for him. He had a tendency to fall into bed with women before he got to know them. He didn't regret having spent time with her. Even if that meant he'd lost out on his chance of getting his hands on those orchids.

There had to be another way to save the Lazy Daze, and he should have thought about that first.

In fact, being with Madison, and hearing her talk about the importance of orchid conservation, listening to the pure passion in her voice when she spoke of the beautiful flowers, brought home the message that his goal was corrupt. He'd known that deep in his heart, but he'd shut down his conscious in order to achieve his goal.

But stealing and smuggling orchids wasn't the way to rescue Deke's ranch. He understood that now. Before meeting by Madison, he'd been very cavalier about the importance of orchids, and now he was ashamed of himself.

Now, all he wanted to do was help her find the orchids.

Not for Deke, not for him, but for her.

He watched her shoulders sag and her eyes mist as she fought back tears, and Jake felt something inside him shift, change.

She had worked and strived and struggled for years to get here, and her dream was slipping from her grasp.

Jake didn't really understand what that was all about. He'd never put that much effort into anything. He skated by, having fun, following his whims, doing as he wished. His fear of deprivation and his need to keep himself entertained had prevented him from searching for deeper meaning.

In Madison, he saw the value of slowing down and taking his time, of being deeply invested in something. Of doing more than skimming the surface of life. Of investing in close human relationships.

He was always on the lookout for fun, always chasing the next thrill. He'd believed staying busy and focusing on happy things were the keys to navigate life's bumps and potholes.

If he were being honest with himself, stealing the orchid had been about more than saving Deke's ranch. The assignment was a challenge, a caper, a great big game just to see if he could do it.

But Madison had made him realize something extremely profound, and to Jake, who was not prone to deep thoughts, it was an earth-shattering insight.

Perhaps that was what this attraction to Madison was all about. An insight into the choices he'd made in his life. Trying to keep himself safe by not being too invested in romantic relationships.

By holding back, holding out, thinking if he kept his heart unfettered, he'd never get hurt the way he'd been damaged as a kid by the parents who'd abandoned him.

This new, and unexpected, self-knowledge rattled Jake to his core. He stared at Madison. His heart filled with so much tenderness that it physically hurt.

There was no way that this relationship could end in anything but disaster. It was all his fault. He's messed up, big time and he couldn't see anyway to change his fate.

An uncharacteristic melancholia stole over him and he had an overwhelming feeling that something—someone—monumental was slipping through his fingers.

"I've been kidding myself." Groaning, she smacked her forehead with a palm.

"Now I wouldn't have expected that from you."

"Expected what?"

"Self-pity."

"I'm not feeling sorry for myself." She paused. "Okay, yes, yes, I am. I've spent three years searching for this orchid, only to be fooled again. I think a little self-pity is allowed."

"C'mon," he said, taking her hand. "We're not giving up yet. Let's keep looking."

"It'll be getting dark soon. We need to make camp for the night."

"Just a little longer," he coaxed.

"All right," she grumbled. "But it's no use."

"What's it gonna hurt?"

She shrugged and followed where he led.

They pushed through the heavy vegetation, fighting against the plants thwarting their progress for what felt like hours, but was probably only fifteen minutes. Humidity plastered their clothes to their skin.

Their backpacks might as well have been lead weights. Jake's shoulders ached, his calves ached, hell, everything ached, and he felt sure Madison was just as miserable, although she looked damn cute in the safari hat of hers and those bright red glasses.

In the distance, they heard a waterfall rushing loudly after the storm. Jake stayed on his toes, not wanting to stumble down a mudslide as they had on their first day in the jungle.

Laboriously, they scaled a small rise and shoved their way through a tunnel of trees where the setting sun flickered in long yellow rays as they entered a small clearing. This was where they'd have to make camp for the night. There wasn't enough daylight left to make it any farther today.

Madison suddenly pulled back on his hand.

"What is it?" he asked, turning to see what had captured her interest.

Jake caught a whiff of her perfect Madison scent and was almost too distracted to pay attention to where she had pointed.

Her breath came in quick, hot pants that warmed the skin on his neck and stirred his lust into something fierce. His gaze fixed on her full sensual lips and the memory of their flavor popped right into his mouth. He studied that small blue vein jumping at her temple. She was excited. Aroused.

And so was he.

"Jake," she whispered. "Look."

At last, he wrenched his gaze from her to find what she was looking at, and it was the most beautiful thing he'd ever seen in his life.

Amore.

Chapter Seven

What Madison saw stole all the air from her lungs. She stood there, mouth agape, heart thumping, mind spinning, senses buzzing.

For there, growing on the surrounding trees, were hundreds of amore orchids stretched out before them. Sweet comets of deep midnight blue and white flowers tangled up among the jungle vines.

Madison had seen many orchids in her life, but none like these. They possessed enormous, long stems and delicate petals that resembled female sex organs. A slow smile spread across her face, and she narrowed her eyes in delight.

Here lay paradise.

"Holy cow. Will you get a load of that?" Jake shook his head.

Simultaneously, they breathed in, inhaling the incredible fragrance of the orchid. It was a merry-go-round of smells—a rose-like scent combined with jasmine, rye bread, musk, wintergreen, cinnamon, cloves.

The odd but enticing chemical combination sent a rush of heat through her nose and into her lungs, warming her blood, sending red-hot waves of desire radiating straight to the tingling spot between her legs.

Amore orchids.

She twirled in a circle, arms outstretched, dizzy, happy.

This was the scent of love. The smell was immediate and undiluted. It needed no words to translate. It smelled like sex.

Madison caught her breath and spun around. Jake was watching her with heavy-lidded eyes, and she knew he felt it, too. This urging, the yearning to be joined.

The look he gave her said, *I can turn your insides into chocolate pudding,* and the cocky tilt to his head left her airless and addled. A deadly combo. This smell. That man.

There was no nerd here. No matter what he pretended, this man was a rebel through and through. A good-time bad boy who wasn't good for her. Another ne'er-do-well. And she knew he was going to lead her into temptation and beyond.

His eyes danced with naughtiness, and when he dropped his backpack, she dropped hers, too. Then he slowly stripped off his black T-shirt, and when she got a good look at his honed, muscled chest, her heart slammed into her ribcage, a car wreck of chaotic sensation.

"C'mere," he said in a husky, dusky voice as ripe as the orchid scent. His expression said he knew her right down to the depths of her soul.

Jake held out his hand.

In a dreamlike state, she moved toward him, pulled by a force she didn't understand but could not resist.

Languidly, he removed her glasses and tucked them into his backpack for safekeeping. He dug around for a condom, and when he found it, he held it up like a great prize.

He stalked back to her, slipped his arms around her, and tugged her down onto the grass in the clearing, kissing her tenderly as if she were as rare and precious as the orchids.

They finished undressing each other. Shoes flying, pants sliding, chastity belt unlocking, until they were totally naked before each other.

He kissed her hard and long and hot. They lay on the slick, wet grass, the sleepy sun filtering through the tree branches. All around them the orchids, heavy and sweet, glowed in that dying light. Under his deft fingers, her aching body bloomed, as spectacular as the flowering plants, and she shivered against his rousing touch.

Lust swamped her. She had to have him. Had to have him or she would surely die. She pulled his bottom lip up between her teeth, and he made a noise of pure enjoyment.

He cupped her face in his palms, then dipped his head and kissed her with a soul-stealing, grade-A, world-class kiss that curled Madison's toes. The moment was brilliant. He was brilliant. It was her most brilliant fantasy come to life.

She burrowed into him, her breasts pressing flush against his muscled chest. He ran his palms up and down her arms. She threw back her head, and he tracked kisses over the tender areas of her throat, nestling and nibbling.

Experimentally, he rubbed his thumbs over her nipples, and they beaded up tight. "Ah," he said. "You like that?"

"Uh-huh." A hazy hotness draped over her, thick with sexual urgency. She wanted him so badly she couldn't speak.

"What about this?" He flicked his tongue along her collarbone.

She shuddered against him.

"And this?" Lightly, he stroked circles on the inside of her arm.

"Beast," she gasped.

"Exactly." He grinned.

The force of his desire caused her to tremble and sweat. Her knees quivered. Her heart pounded.

He tunneled his fingers through her hair. She felt his presence in every cell of her body.

He loved her with his mouth, tonguing her with amazing tenderness, a slow glide from the sensitive spot behind her knee, around to her kneecap, and up her inner thigh until she was rolling in ecstasy.

She floated, bodiless. She was total awareness, her entire being a giant throb of sexual energy.

He kissed lazy circles of heat, and she was transfixed. Finally, he edged to the spot where she wanted him to be, at the sweet *V* between her legs.

His wet tongue teased, slowly licking her outer lips. Inhaled her. Then caressed her with the sensuous sweep of his tongue.

He sucked at every fold, lapped at her ridges, and lifted her buttocks to devour his meal. An electric flash of brilliant energy lit the inside of her head, and all the air was drained from her lungs.

She surfed his tongue, owned it. She hovered on the brink of orgasm, but he would not let her fall over. A steady strumming vibration began deep in her throat, emerging as a wild moan.

She thrust herself against his mouth, gripping the sides of his head with her thighs, letting her juices flow.

He released her but didn't remove his tongue from her twitching body. His tongue danced with her, wriggling nimbly.

Her skin was incredibly sensitive, her body tingling and tender. She tried to push him away—it was simply too much pleasure—but he stayed put, pushing his tongue deep inside her. Then out and down to the region beyond.

This new sensation drove her into a frenzy. Her muscles flexed. Blinding flashes of light. A rushing sound like ocean waves in her head. Uncontrollable spasms rattled her body.

Her world quaked.

His fingers touched and tickled and tingled. Her butt and her inner thigh. He slid one finger deep inside her wetness, while his tongue continued to strum the feminine head of her.

She didn't know where she was or who she was with. Who was she? Woman or creature?

His hands were broad and warm. His mouth was an instrument of exquisite torture. Time spun, morphed, as elusive as space.

She was spellbound, mesmerized, entranced. Embraced by a longing so precious and severe she couldn't breathe. In delicious anguish, she cried out her delight.

He rocked back on his heels, clasped her to his chest, and held her tight, his hands threaded in her hair, until her crazy thudding heart calmed.

Then, when she had rested, he made love to her again, sinking his flesh into hers. He wanted her as desperately as she wanted him, with the same high-octane intensity.

As their bodies joined and hotly fused in the moonlight—at some point the sun had gone down, and the moon had appeared—orchid pollen traveled on the air, floating on the night breeze. The petals rustled, their minute fluttering as primal as the heavy breathing Madison and Jake shared.

As the twilight deepened, the flowers took on an ethereal glow, shining white in the dimming light.

Scent drenched the air—orchids and mating—combining, fusing, part of an ancient dance as old as the sun and the moon and the stars.

The entire time he was buried inside her, he stared into her eyes as if he were lost in her gaze and could not find his way out. Did not even want to find his way out.

Two became one.

A single being.

Trembling and clinging.

His shaft filled her up, pushing far inside her until he could go no farther.

Then he pulled back. In and out, he moved in an even tempo that rocked her soul. He rode her, and she rode him until they both came in a blazing, blinding light.

A WHILE LATER, JAKE awoke and listened to Maddie's soft breathing. Her head was resting on his chest, and it felt so good he smiled into the darkness.

And then he remembered why he was in Costa Rica.

He had a secret to confess. Something he should have told her before he made love to her, but he'd been so caught up in the moment, so under her spell, so excited for her over the discovery of the amore orchids that he'd followed his instincts and not his head.

Like always.

Except everything else was different here, and his usual behavior no longer applied. Not with Maddie. With her, he wouldn't have to look for adventure or scout out the next thrill. She was the adventure, being with her the thrill. He just prayed she'd forgive him when he told her the truth.

"Jake?" she whispered into the sultry darkness.

"Uh-huh."

"Do you have any more condoms?"

"Yes."

She walked her fingers up his chest. "Could we um... go again?"

Now's the time, speak!

He was going to. He intended to, but then she was touching her hot, sweet tongue to his nipple, and all conscious thought flew right out of his brain. He searched for the condom, found it, got it on somehow, then rolled over, taking her with him, cradling Madison in his arms.

She let out a soft little moan and opened her legs.

He held his weight on his forearms and slid into her welcoming wetness. Overhead, the moon shone down on her face. He stared into her bright, trusting eyes and moved his body over hers, fitting perfectly against the curved hollow of her hips.

Maddie caressed his face with her tender hands and murmured endearments in a lyrical tone. But soon the hushed whispers turned to gritty groans and heated gasps. She made him feel like the best lover on earth.

He loved hearing her sexy sounds. In fact, he was pretty sure he could listen to them for the rest of his life and die a happy, happy man.

And when her release came, he twined their hands together above her head and rocked into her with one fierce thrust. She arched her back, eager to meet him, and wrapped her legs around his waist, pulling him in as deep as he could go. Their fingers were locked, their gazes welded as they came in one shattering shudder.

"Wow," she breathed a few minutes after they'd come spiraling down. "Just wow."

"That doesn't begin to cover it."

They were lying on their backs, their eyes directed up at the vast field of stars, wrapped in a cocoon of amore-orchid scent.

"That was the best," she whispered.

"For me, too," he confessed.

"I will never forget this moment for as long as I live."

"Me too."

"It was...you were...you make me feel so..."

He waited for her to finish, wondering how he made her feel, when the steady sounds of her breathing told him she'd fallen asleep.

Jake smiled. He'd worn her out.

He marveled at how he could be so connected to someone he'd only known for four days. It made no sense, but he couldn't deny it.

Could he be... was he possibly... falling in love?

Chapter Eight

Madison woke just after dawn.

Jake lay next to her, snoring lightly.

Grinning, she levered herself up on one elbow and stared down at him.

His tousled hair curled across his forehead. In repose, his firm jaw seemed softer. The man was fricking gorgeous. How had she snagged a guy like him?

You didn't snag him. This was just a fantasy come true for one night. Read no more into it than that.

It sounded good as a theory, but she greedily wanted more.

Be real. You're working on your doctorate. You live in New York. And he...

Suddenly, she realized she didn't even know what he did for a living. Whenever she'd asked, he had glibly changed the subject in that smooth way of his.

Uneasiness skittered over her. Another ne'er-do-well. Boy, could she pick 'em or what?

Well, he'd distracted her long enough; she had orchids to catalogue. Where were her glasses? Oh, yeah, he'd put them in his backpack. She eased to her feet, gathered up her clothes, hurriedly dressed, and then went to retrieve her spectacles.

She dug around on top of the backpack and didn't see them. She pushed aside his change of clothes and the last of their food supplies, and that's when she found it.

The six-inch harvesting knife. A pair of stainless-steel scissors. A bottle of root stimulator and an instruction book on how to transplant and transport orchids.

Her blood ran icy. She stared at the items, praying she wasn't seeing what she was seeing. Hoping there was a perfectly innocent explanation for why he was toting these things around with him but knowing in her heart of hearts there wasn't.

"Maddie."

She spun around, the treacherous items in her hands.

Jake was on his feet, standing naked, completely exposed, a guilty expression on his face. "I can explain."

Madison felt sick to her stomach. "You're not a flower enthusiast. You're an orchid thief. A smuggler."

He raised a finger. "Small point, I'm not an orchid thief or a smuggler. At least not yet. I came here to become one, yes, but I didn't do it."

Horrified, she stared at him. "Who are you?"

"I train cutting horses."

She looked confused. "You're a cowboy?"

Actually, it made total sense. He had a lanky, muscular body that fit the job.

"I am."

"Why are you stealing orchids?"

"I was blackmailed into by a man whose cutting horse I train. He's a billionaire international importer/exporter and I train his cutting horses—"

"What did you do?"

"Huh?"

"What's he holding over your head. How are you so desperate to sink so low?" She curled her upper lip, disgusted with Jake and herself.

"The billionaire has got my foster father over a barrel. Deke was going to lose his family ranch if I didn't agree to Mr. Lui's scheme to steal the amore orchid from you guys."

"Mr. Lui. That's his name?"

Jake nodded, looking as miserable as Madison felt. "I'm sorry. I didn't fully understand."

"You didn't understand what you were doing was a crime?"

"I knew it was illegal, I just thought it was no big deal. I mean, it is just a flower.... Or it was until I got to know you and you made me understand just how important the orchid is. I did not know."

"You're a guy who has no trouble massaging the truth. Pretending to be interested in botany, purposefully targeting me—" She broke off. Shivered. Suddenly bone deep cold despite the oppressive heat.

She threw her head back and yelled her agony at the sky. "I can't believe this is happening to me again. This one is the ne'er-do-well to end all ne'er-do-wells. What is it?" She threw out her arms. "Am I a ne'er-do-well magnet?"

He grabbed his jeans and jammed his legs into them. "Maddie, you gotta listen to me. I did have bad intentions when I initially came on this trip, but after meeting you, getting to know you and the way you love orchids... I've known no one as passionate about anything as you are. I had already changed my mind and decided I wouldn't steal the orchids. I was going to find another way to save Deke's ranch."

"You expect me to believe that cock-and-bull story?"

"I can't control what you believe, but it's the truth."

"Oh, the altruistic orchid thief."

He came toward her and reached out a hand, pure regret written across his face. "I'm so very sorry."

She spun away from him. "Do not touch me. Don't you dare touch me."

"Last night was—"

"No. You don't get to tug on my heartstrings. Last night was a huge mistake. *Huge*." She was so angry that she couldn't figure out how to express her rage without completely losing it. "You used me."

"Only at first. Once I got to know you, things changed."

The pain in her heart was so acute she could barely catch her breath. She'd been hurt before, but she'd never felt as utterly betrayed as she did right now.

"Go. Leave. Get out of my sight." She pointed a trembling finger. "I can't stand to look at you one second longer."

"THIS LOOKS REALLY BAD, Maddie," he said. "I know it does, but we can get past this if you can find it in your heart to forgive me. I can change. I want to change."

"You're a thief, a smuggler, a mercenary, a liar and a cheat!"

"Yes, maybe I am all those things, but you make me want to be a better man. Please—"

She cut him off. "You don't care about these precious orchids, and you don't care about me. You're a thief and a smuggler."

He deserved it, Jake understood that, but it killed his soul that she believed he'd intentionally set out to hurt her.

"I can't believe I lost the no-sex bet over the likes of you." She gritted her teeth.

The anger in her eyes tore at his heart. She hated him. Madison wasn't interested in hearing a single word he had to say, and he couldn't blame her.

He felt as if he were shrinking, growing smaller every second, losing any self-respect he might have possessed. His loosey-goosey values had led him here. He'd allowed his need for fun and excitement and adventure and the thrill of the chase to override his common sense. Sure, he'd done it to save the ranch for Deke, but there were other ways to get money. He should have explored them all before agreeing to Lui's nefarious scheme.

If he was being honest with himself, he'd admit he'd accepted the job from Liu for the challenge. Madison was right. He was all the things she'd called him—a thief, a smuggler, a mercenary, a cheat and a liar.

"I want you to pack up your things and leave this instant," she said, her voice as cold as an arctic breeze.

"Mad—"

She pointed toward base camp. "If you go now, I won't tell the authorities you were here since you didn't have time to steal an orchid. It's a far better deal than you deserve. I'd take it if I were you."

"I can't leave you in the jungle alone."

"She's not alone," a male voice said from behind them.

Jake spun around to see Professor Hampton, Bunk, Lucinda, and all the other volunteers glaring at him as if he was scum of the earth.

"Madison might not turn you over to the authorities," Hampton said. "But I sure as hell will."

Chapter Nine

Since Jake hadn't stolen the orchids or tried to smuggle them, the authorities couldn't really hold him, although they red flagged his passport and informed Jake that he was no longer welcome in Costa Rica.

As a show of goodwill, he gave them Liu's name as an orchid collector to watch out for. Now he could add rat fink to his long list of sins.

With a heavy heart, he flew home to Texas.

He'd brought this on himself. He'd been glib and cavalier. He'd taken life too lightly. He hadn't considered the consequences of his actions.

But he was sure considering them now. He'd been so close to something truly wonderful, and by being deceptive, he'd let it all slip through his fingers.

It was a wake-up call. He thought of the amore orchid, almost the navy blue of Madison's eyes. Dark and soulful. Growing deep in the jungle. A rare and unique beauty nearly impossible to find.

Once he was on American soil, Jake called Mr. Liu and told him not only was the deal off, but that the amore orchid was probably going on the endangered species list soon, and he would no longer train Lui's cutting horses.

Liu cursed both in English and Taiwanese, throwing around empty threats.

Jake didn't care. He had bigger fish to fry. Like helping Deke keep Lui from foreclosing on the Lazy Daze.

And he had to come up with a plan to win Madison back, although deep inside he feared he was beyond redemption in her eyes.

A smarter man would just let things lie and move on with his life.

Jake arrived at the Lazy Daze feeling lighter from having just told off Liu. He hadn't warned Deke that he was coming home, and he was surprised to see a "sold" sign on the property.

What was going on? Had Lui foreclosed despite sending Jake after the orchid? That sonofabitch.

Confused, Jake pulled his pickup truck into the driveway just as when Deke came around the side of the house, whistling happily.

"Jake!" Deke exclaimed, and his eyes lit up. He clasped him in a warm embrace. "When did you get back from Costa Rica?"

"Just now."

"Why didn't you call me?"

Jake shrugged. "I guess I was too embarrassed."

"Embarrassed about what?"

"Can we go inside and talk?" Jake drank in the man who was the only family he'd ever known. Stocky, balding, but still in good shape for a man his age. Deke had a lot of good years left in him.

"Sure, sure. C'mon it." Deke led him inside the house to the kitchen. "You hungry?"

"No, no, I'm fine. What's that real estate sign in the yard about?"

Deke went to the fridge, pulled out two beers. Twisted the caps off both bottles and passed one to Jake.

"Thanks." Jake took the beer, even though he didn't really want it. "Lui foreclosed?"

"Nope, I sold the Lazy Daze, so I could pay that tyrant and get him out of my life. I was such an idiot to take a loan from him."

"Deke! I'm so sorry you lost your family place."

"Don't look so distraught, Jake. It's just a piece of land."

"But the Lazy Daze was your life."

"And it tied me down 24/7 for my whole life."

"But... but... I thought you loved the homestead."

"I do. I did. But after losing Margie, it got old. Especially once you were grown. I kept the ranch for as long as I did because you enjoyed coming back here to train horses. But after the pandemic hit and no one could go on vacation, it was a sign for me to close the dude ranch. I'm not getting any younger, kiddo, and if I want to have a few adventures of my own before I die, I realized the time is now."

"Wow." Jake blinked at the man who'd raised him.

Here he'd been thinking losing the dude ranch would break Deke's heart, but he seemed happier than Jake had ever seen him.

"But you were so upset when you told me you were going to have to sell because Lui was calling in the note."

"I'm not saying it didn't hurt. Growth always hurts. But you can't move forward until you let go of the past. I'm ready to step into a bright new future. What about you?"

Jake told him then. About Liu and the amore orchid, about Madison and the mess he'd made in Costa Rica. He held nothing back.

When he was finished, a smile tipped the corners of Deke's lips.

"This funny to you, Deke?"

"Not funny." Deke's eyes danced with amusement. "Inevitable."

"Inevitable that my recklessness would lead me to trouble?"

"Inevitable that you would fall in love."

"Nah…" Jake shook his head. "I'm not in love."

"You sure?"

"Yeah." He nodded. "You think?"

"Only one thing could make you take a hard look at your life and reevaluate it to this degree. And when you talk about Madison, your entire face lights up the way mine did with Margie. Cowboy, I'd say you're stone cold in love."

Chapter Ten

Madison had always assumed that finding the amore orchid would be the greatest moment of her life.

It wasn't.

She took no joy in it because, for some cursed reason, all she could think about was Jake. Yes, he'd duped her. Yes, he'd had bad intentions. But in the end, he hadn't stolen the orchids.

That's because you caught him before he had a chance.

She remembered the way he'd looked in the jungle, standing before her, completely baring his heart. Vulnerable, begging her forgiveness, and a lump of despair scaled her throat.

Madison believed him. Believed he'd recognized that he'd made a mistake, admitted it, and was truly remorseful.

But she'd been so hurt that she hadn't been able to get past her own pain and offer him the forgiveness he had clearly wanted.

She'd been back from her trip for two weeks, teaching the second half of the summer school session for Hampton. Her professor was still in Costa Rica, soaking up the glory for having discovered the amore, barely giving her any credit at all beyond mumbling to the press that her calculations about soil nitrogen levels in that region led him to the area. What had she expected from a raging egomaniac?

Men. She was sick of them all.

"Hey, Ms. Garrett," one of the male students said, yanking her distracted thoughts back to the present.

She blinked at the small group of summer school students seated before her. "Yes?"

"I heard on the news this morning that a Taiwanese billionaire was charged with hiring orchid smugglers to steal rare orchids from around the world."

"Oh? I hadn't heard that."

"What do you think about the practice of orchid smuggling?" the student asked.

"It's a travesty," she said.

"C'mon, honestly, what's the big deal? I mean, it's just a flower. It's not like it is drugs or anything."

Madison launched into a lecture on why the illegal trafficking of orchids was detrimental on so many levels, but in the back of her mind, she kept considering what the student had said.

When the class was over, she dismissed the students and bent to collect her things to get out of the way for the next class. She heard footsteps in the auditorium, but she figured it was just a student coming back for something they'd forgotten.

Until a deep masculine voice said, "How you doin', Maddie?"

She whirled around, her heart pounding.

Jake stood there looking deadly handsome and uncharacteristically serious, she felt her grip loosen on the books and papers in her hand, felt them tumble to the floor.

Madison stood frozen, unable to move to pick them up, pinned to the spot by Jake's wistful gaze.

"What are you doing here?"

"I came to see you." He sauntered toward her.

"Well, I don't want to see you. I thought I made that clear enough in Costa Rica."

"You did." He nodded, coming up onto the lectern stage with her. "But I can't stay away. I know I hurt you, and I'm sorrier than words can ever say. I hope you'll give me a chance to make it up to you."

"Why should I?" She crossed her arms over her chest to protect her melting heart.

"I've already made a start," he said.

"You turned Liu in? I saw on the news where he's in hot water."

"Yes, I did. Someone taught me the importance of protecting the orchids. I understand now how inconsiderate I've been." Still holding her gaze, he reached out to take her hand, interlacing their fingers. "That someone also taught me something else."

"What's that?" she asked in a low tone, wanting so badly to believe him.

"I'm never going to find love if I keep running from it."

"No?" She felt the breath leave her body.

"Love comes from the heart, Maddie. And my heart is right here."

Her pulse leapt crazily. "What are you saying, Jake?"

"These kinds of feelings don't come along every day, and I think we owe it to ourselves to see where this might lead."

"I'm sorry, but I promised myself I would never get involved with any more ne'er-do-wells. And poaching is a big deal to me."

"Then you're in luck."

"Oh?" What was he talking about?

"From now on, I'm going to be an always-do-well. I'm doing my best to make amends, and I hope you'll give me a chance to prove it to you."

"You're going to change?" She snapped her fingers. "Just like that?"

"I'm going to try. I've given up training cutting horses."

"Why?"

"My foster father sold his dude ranch."

"Lui foreclosed on it?"

"No. Deke sold it to pay off Lui. Now, he gets to have the life he's been longing for."

"Doing what?"

"Kicking back at the beach."

"So what are you going to do if you're not training cutting horses?"

"Eco-tourism."

"Huh?"

"Your passion for orchids got me worked up, and I took a job. I'll be working for a company based here in New York that sends out experienced guides to lead conservation-minded individuals interested in doing their part in preserving endangered species."

"Really?"

"Really."

They stared at each other for a very long time.

"Can you find it in your heart to forgive me, Maddie?"

"You're serious about this?"

"Maddie, I'd do *anything* to redeem myself in your eyes. You've shown me the error of my ways, and I'm praying you won't just write me off."

"I guess there's no sense in being a hard-ass," she whispered, wanting so much to forgive him. "I think I can give you another chance."

Relief crossed his face, immediately replaced by the impish grin she knew so well. "Hey, I need a hard-ass to make me toe the line, but from what I remember, your fanny is not too hard, not too soft, but just right."

"Oh, ho?"

He reached out to splay a palm to her backside. "You keep me on my toes, Madison Garrett, and it's one of the thing I love most about you. I need someone like you in my life."

"And you keep me from being too much in my head. You ground me, Jake."

"Who knew," he murmured, lowering his head to steal a kiss, "that the freewheeling cowboy and the calculating professor would be a perfect match?"

"Who knew?" she echoed and kissed him back.

"Now about that heart-shaped birthmark you teased me with…. It was too dark in the jungle for me to find it that night we made love. Are you ever going to show it to me in the light of day?"

She glanced toward the door, saw they were alone, then coyly raised her shirt and inched down the waistband of her pants to reveal the birthmark on her backside.

"I spy with my little eye something very sweet," he murmured.

Then Maddie took him back to her apartment, showed him her bedroom with photographs of the amore orchid she'd taken in Costa Rica, and there, with the smell of passion in the air, they made love all night long.

AND THEN THERE WERE two.

Check out the third book in the Cowboy Rendezvous series, *Cody*.

DEAR READER,

Readers are an author's lifeblood, and the stories couldn't happen without you. Thank you so much for reading, you are important.

If you enjoyed *Jake* I would so appreciate a review. You have no idea how much it means.

If you'd like to keep up with my latest releases, you can sign up for my newsletter @ https://loriwilde.com/subscribe/

To check out other books, you can visit me on the web @ www.loriwilde.com[1].

Much love and light to you!

Lori

---

1.   http://www.loriwilde.com/

Don't miss out!

Visit the website below and you can sign up to receive emails whenever Lori Wilde publishes a new book. There's no charge and no obligation.

https://books2read.com/r/B-A-BAEH-NLSXB

BOOKS 2 READ

Connecting independent readers to independent writers.

Did you love *Jake*? Then you should read *Cody*² by Lori Wilde!

Cowboy Cody Colton was once Emma Jacobs' unrequited high school crush but then she got a scholarship to NYU and bid goodbye to small town Texas and hello to big city lights.

Now a children's librarian, Emma is an urbanite through and through and she would rather have a root canal than camp in a tent, but when she finds herself hoodwinked into a Colorado whitewater rafting trip, she figures at least she's a shoo-in to win the "summer-of-no-sex" celibacy² wager she's made with her three best friends.

---

2. https://books2read.com/u/mV8g6l

3. https://books2read.com/u/mV8g6l

That is until she learns the lanky cowboy serving as their wilderness guide is none other than Cody Colton and he's suddenly looking at Emma in a whole new light...

Read more at https://loriwilde.com.

Also by Lori Wilde

Cowboy Confidential
Cowboy Cop
Cowboy Protector
Cowboy Bounty Hunter
Cowboy Bodyguard
Cowboy Outlaw

Cowboy Rendezvous
Tomaz
Jake
Cody

Heartthrob Hospital
The Thunderbolt
The Jinx
The Hotshot

Kringle, Texas
A Perfect Christmas Gift
A Perfect Christmas Wish
A Perfect Christmas Surprise
A Perfect Christmas Joy
A Perfect Christmas Reunion

One Scorching Summer
Mr. Temptation
Mr. Temptation
Mr. Intoxicating
Mr. Undeniable
Mr. Scandalous

Texas Rascals
Keegan
Texas Rascals Three Book Collection
Matt
Texas Rascals Three Book Collection
Nick
Kurt
Tucker
Kael
Truman
Brodie

Dan
Rex
Clay
Jonah

Watch for more at https://loriwilde.com.

About the Author

Lori Wilde is the New York Times, USA Today and Publishers' Weekly bestselling author of 85 works of romantic fiction. She's a three time Romance Writers' of America RITA finalist and has four times been nominated for Romantic Times Readers' Choice Award. She has won numerous other awards as well. Her books have been translated into 26 languages, with more than four million copies of her books sold worldwide. Her breakout novel, The First Love Cookie Club, has been optioned for a TV movie.

Lori is a registered nurse with a BSN from Texas Christian University. She holds a certificate in forensics, and is also a certified yoga instructor.

A fifth generation Texan, Lori lives with her husband, Bill, in the Cutting Horse Capital of the World; where they run

Epiphany Orchards, a writing/creativity retreat for the care and enrichment of the artistic soul.

Read more at https://loriwilde.com.